Sentimental
JOURNEY

An Illustrated Time Travel Romance

BY LINDA LAUREN

Gonna take a Sentimental Journey,
Gonna set my heart at ease.
Gonna make a Sentimental Journey,
to renew old memories.

Copyright 1944 by Morley Music Co., Inc.

Copyright Renewed 1971.

All Rights Reserved.

ISBN: 0615686141

ISBN 13: 9780615686141

Library of Congress Control Number: 2012947433
Embracing The Universe

In Loving Memory

To my parents, Frances & Jerry Gialanella

Their stories brought to life the youthful, naïve exuberance of a generation embracing a second world war and showed me the romance behind the reality.

I began this novel back in 1992 when they were both still with us, but I did not return to it until recently. This book is in keeping with a promise that I would use their first names as characters.

I hope they like it!

In Gratitude

This particular time travel holds a very dear place in my heart because it is a direct result of memories my late mother shared with me regarding her meeting, being courted by, and marrying my father. I am grateful for that firsthand knowledge.

The 1944 lapel watch pin described and pictured in the book belonged to my mother, and I have a photo of her wearing it. She gave it to me when I started writing this story to help me develop the plot. I still have it, and it keeps perfect time. Because of this, I have written the story in the time travel style of the late Jack Finney who gave us the classic illustrated novel *Time and Again*. It is my hope that the photographs will lend the sense of time and place for the reader to experience.

The photos were gleaned from my personal photo albums, and any additional information was taken from various taped recordings, family contributions, videos, and conversations that occurred over the years. Special thanks to my cousins Bob and Beth Monica for providing me with photos of Bob's parents (my real life godparents, Jeanne and Joey Monica) as well as a wonderful photo of my parents in the 1940s, so that I may add to the historic value of the telling of this particular time travel. The Leg Makeup Bar photo is courtesy of Getty Images.

I have been blessed with the love and friendship of people who are family to me, now that my parents are dancing in that nightclub in the sky, and I want to take this opportunity to thank Susan Dolinko, Todd Evans, Jeffrey Moran, and their little pooch, Grace. Your love and support has seen me through incredible times, and I am grateful to share my life with people of strong spiritual love.

To my extended family, clients, friends, and all those wonderful people I have yet to meet, I thank you for picking this book as part of your reading experience, and I hope I meet your expectations.

God bless,

Linda Lauren
West Orange & Mountainside, NJ
Autumn 2014

Dedication

*To my little furry roommates, Gidget and Cosmo:
you are the best little companions anyone could ask for!
Thank you for your love and patience while I was writing.*

I love you.

CHAPTER ONE

December 1992
ChemProbe Auditorium, NYC

"Ah...CHOO!"

Allison McKay slipped a hand into the pocket of her blazer, drew out a well-worn tissue, and blew into it. With shaking hands she picked up her hastily prepared speech and looked out from the podium of the ChemProbe auditorium at the one hundred hand-selected members of the media who gathered to hear her presentation. Though the words were right in front of her in crystal-clear type, they blurred indistinctly when she attempted to read them through her watery, red eyes. This cold had gotten the better of her, and she wished she could have backed out of the presentation. But that wasn't going to happen. As head of public relations, it was her responsibility to personally make this announcement. For several years Dr. Horace Banks had had a media lock on this particular project, and few people had been trusted.

The low chatter of the people seated in the front rose up above a murmur, and the anticipation in the room made Allison feel even more uncomfortable. Stuffing the tissue back into her pocket, she looked up once again into the audience and cleared her throat uncomfortably.

"Though research is still in its infancy, Doctors Horace Banks and Robin Page of ChemProbe Creative Labs have been working on a possible cure for the common cold."

Allison waited for the expected audible awe and was not disappointed. She reached over to pick up a vial containing a red, white, and blue capsule and held it up for view. "This time-release capsule will function much the same way as any other over-the-counter medication with a time-release effect. Laboratory tests with Zelda the chimp have been successful enough to warrant disclosure to the public."

"When will they be able to test this capsule on a human?" A young man stood, notebook and pen in hand.

Allison felt the second sneeze claim her, and the tissue flew to her swollen nostrils.

"Ah…CHOO!"

I'm not going to get through this. She cast a pleading look to Robin Page who was standing off in the wings, waiting his turn. He immediately mounted the steps to the stage to join her at the podium.

"Thank you, Ms. McKay." Robin shook her hand. "I can take over from here."

He passed a hand over her shoulder as she left the stage, and she watched him a moment from the sidelines, taking command in his assuming way, his tall, muscular body lending detail to his neatly tailored blue suit. She smiled and turned toward the Exit sign leading to the cafeteria.

Thirty-five with sandy hair and deep-blue eyes, the very single Dr. Robin Page was handsome and eligible, but he was also too concentrated and intense about his work. He kept long hours in the lab and opted for naps on the couch in the doctor's solarium rather than to go home. The woman who made the mistake of losing her heart to Robin Page was in for a great deal of loneliness.

Allison sat down with a cup of cafeteria coffee and blew her nose twice more. Never did she remember a cold overwhelming her so completely as this one. It had been three weeks now, and she couldn't find relief.

"Ah...CHOO!"

"God bless you." Robin joined her at the small round table and loosened his tie. "It's Horace's turn at the podium; I've fielded enough questions. Journalists can be a persistent bunch." He gave out a long sigh and smiled. "How are you feeling?"

Allison looked up at him through puffy eyes. "Depressed. I've never been sick this long." She drained the rest of the coffee from the Styrofoam cup and peeled away the rim with impatient fingers. "I wish you and Horace *had* made a human breakthrough with the capsule," she sniffled. "I'd gladly offer myself to the experiment."

"I'm sure you would." Robin smiled warmly and touched a hand to hers. "Don't let this cold intimidate you." He reached into the breast pocket of his jacket for his prescription pad and wrote quickly. "Have this filled." He handed her the slip of paper. "A good dose of antibiotics is what you need."

"Thanks." She folded the prescription and tucked it into her purse.

"Now go home and get some rest."

Allison got up and tossed the tattered cup into the trash, offering Robin a limp wave on her way out.

CHAPTER TWO

On the way home, Allison stopped at the corner drug store. The pharmacist said there would be a considerable wait for her prescription. Her patience having run out long ago, she searched the shelves for a box of cold capsules that had worked in the past, purchased it, and told the pharmacist she'd be back later.

Walking quickly up her street, Allison did her best to dodge the littered garbage and boozy comments from loitering homeless people who had taken up temporary residence. The city that had once drawn her so magically to it now instilled real fear in her; the faded, dirty color of the buildings were depressing in contrast to what they once were.

"Hey, baby, can you spare a buck?" One of the men touched her shoulder, and she immediately jerked away and walked briskly up the steps of the brownstone.

Safely inside the front door, she stood in the corridor a few moments to catch her breath—the breath of fear and repulsion—and loosened the buttons of her long down jacket.

"Ah...CHOO!" She pulled out yet another tissue and blew into it.

"Allison?" Frances Giovani opened her door slowly and poked out her dyed-red head before stepping into the hallway. "Never can tell who's lurking about," she announced, her arthritic hands fumbling with the buttons of her blue smock. "A shame what's happened to this city. Nothing like the good old days."

Even though Allison couldn't identify with those good old days, she nodded. "Days like today I hate this city...this time we live in," she said, her long, dark hair damp and trailing down her back, the bangs sticking to her forehead in sweat.

"Still got your cold, I see. How did your presentation go today?"

Allison smiled. Frances was like the neighborhood mom to her, and they often had long talks about Allison's work. Frances was one of those rare people who could keep things to herself, and it was easy for Allison to confide in her.

"It made me wish I could take one of those capsules to get rid of my own cold."

"Then Zelda is improving?"

"The experiments are going well. Now that the media is involved I don't think ChemProbe should have a problem acquiring additional funds for the project."

"Imagine how wonderful it would be to find a cure for the common cold!"

"Ah...CHOO!" Allison nodded again and blew into the remnants of her tissue.

"I'll fix you some chicken soup and bring it up later."

"You'll get no argument from me. Thanks."

Thrice bolting the door to her apartment on the third floor, Allison flung her coat over the sofa and headed for the bedroom where she sank her aching body onto the soft mattress.

I don't know how much more of this miserable cold I can take.

She sat up and dumped the contents of her purse onto the bed in search of the cold capsules she had picked up at the pharmacy. Next to the box was the test tube, and in it, a way out of this misery. Carefully pulling at the rubber stopper, Allison spilled the capsule into her hand. *What if?* No...not without supervision. The doctors would be furious, and ChemProbe could face a possible lawsuit.

"Ah...CHOO!"

Allison grabbed another tissue and stared desperately down at the capsule again. Without further hesitation, she reached over for the water pitcher on the night table and poured a full glass. She brought the capsule to her lips, sipped the water...and swallowed.

CHAPTER THREE

Allison was floating, riding waves as she tossed and turned, a seasickness taking hold of her. She opened her eyes and was met with a film that prevented her from seeing anything more than a shadow. She blinked and rubbed them before slowly straining them into focus.

Make Love, Not War proclaimed the poster on the wall across from the bed in loud Day-Glo colors. The rest of the room was wallpapered in tiny rosebuds that were far from soothing.

Wait…rosebud wallpaper? And what is that poster doing there?

She opened her eyes wider, then squinted. Pressing a hand down on the mattress for support, Allison raised her body up and felt a wave move underneath her. The wave made her unsteady and uncomfortable, and it seemed to follow her as she moved to gain her footing. Allison looked down and smoothed her hand over the bedding. It was not she who floated, but the bed. A waterbed. The problem was that Allison didn't own a waterbed, or a Day-Glo poster for that matter! And her bedroom was pale pink, not floral.

"Where the hell am I?" She struggled out of the drifting bed and moved with stocking feet to the brown wooden beads hanging in the doorway and pushed them noisily aside.

More sounds...music...*The Doors first album?* And then a smell—a mixture of what she could only describe as sweet and sour—thickly permeated the air. She recognized both: marijuana and incense. *Patchouli?* Dizzy and disoriented, Allison carefully walked into the living room. Four people sat cross-legged on the floor, a smoking hookah in the center of them. She tried to speak, but the words would not come. The other people in the room were quite animated—two men and two women, all with hair trailing down their backs. Their heated topic was the war in Vietnam, and for some reason the scene was a familiar one.

"I tell you, we have no business being there," one of the young men passionately declared. "There is simply no sense to it!"

Allison combed her fingers through her hair, her brown eyes wide with confusion. None of this is real, she told herself. I'm in a dream…or a nightmare from the looks of this place.

"What the hell is going on here?" she shouted, finding her voice to test the theory.

The group ignored her as they continued in heated debate. Allison bent down and touched the shoulder of the doe-eyed girl who was stringing beads next to the young man who led the conversation.

Allison's hand went right through her!

"Well, isn't this an interesting situation," she said.

Allison looked down at the girl's completed pile of beads and picked up the bright-blue necklace on top. Steady and solid, it remained in her hands. Quickly, she slid them into the pocket of her pants. The look of astonishment and horror on Doe-eye's face made Allison laugh. "You can't see me, but you saw those love beads move through the air and — POOF — vanish!" Laughing herself to tears, Allison leaned against the wall for support.

"You spooked or something?" The young man waved a hand in front of Doe-eyes.

"Didn't you see it?" she questioned in a small trembling voice.

"What?" he asked while drawing on the long end of the pipe.

"Don't tell me you didn't see it!" Doe-eyes looked to the others. "My love beads…the blue ones that were on top of the pile. They flew in the air and disappeared!"

"You're stoned," the other girl answered. "You sure you didn't take that tab of Orange Sunshine we can't seem to find?"

"Yeah," the young man agreed. "You only hallucinate when you've been doing acid."

"I swear I'm not tripping! Someone took my beads! Why won't you believe me?"

Still laughing, Allison reluctantly attempted to pull herself together. As she moved from the wall, her hair caught on something behind her, and she turned. A calendar sporting peace sign artwork hung on a nail.

November 1969? This is some dream!

No wonder it was a familiar scene. She was an active two-year-old in 1969, always in her parents' way and never allowed in the room where they got high, which, she noticed, was similar to this one but smaller. But Allison remembered it just the same, as she would peer through a crack in the partially open bedroom door of her house and watch them, her head spinning slightly from the fumes coming from the funny-smelling room. Allison had always been intrigued by that smell. *Smell?* She inhaled deeply through clear nostrils; the only water in her eyes the tears of laughter. Her cold was completely gone.

CHAPTER FOUR

Twenty-four hours later, Allison opened her eyes to the soft pink walls of her own bedroom. To make sure, she sat up and felt the mattress for firmness. Thank God, it wasn't a waterbed. She laughed. *What a crazy dream that was!* Maybe ChemProbe had mistakenly made a pill that helped induce lucid dreams, she thought, her hands still pressing on the mattress in awe at the continued confirmation of the dream. Rather than feeling refreshed, Allison felt completely drained. It was as if she had gotten no sleep at all. She drew the covers up and leaned back against the soft pillows. She heard something drop when she did and bent over the side of the bed. The blue love beads lay on the pink rug in a tangled mass.

It wasn't as dream? Those are travelin' love beads...the same ones I took from Doe-eyes' pile...in 1969!

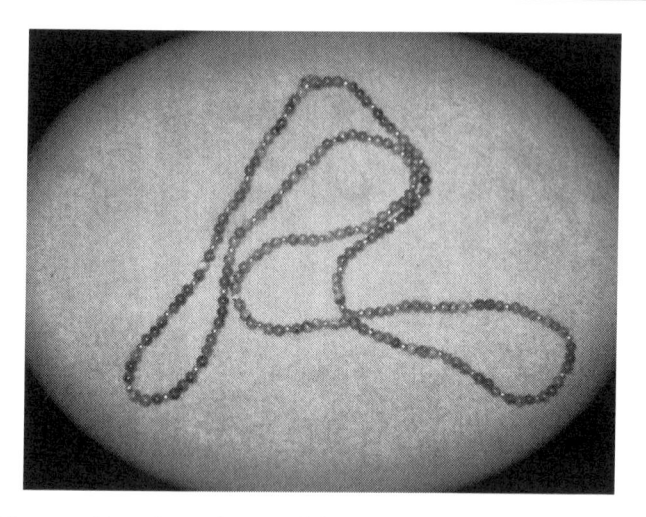

The realization claimed her immediately: the ChemProbe capsule was time release all right, and it managed to do just that...release actual time.

The thought suddenly alarmed her. If this was true, she wondered how it was affecting Zelda at the lab. How would an animal be able to cope with traveling through time? Was the capsule reliable? Was Zelda able to keep going back to the same time and place, or was she moving through time and/or the present without control or direction? There were so many questions the experience left to be answered.

"Allison!" A frantic Mrs. G. was banging at the apartment door, and Allison rushed out of bed to answer. Disengaging the locks, she opened the door to find Frances Giovani in a red warm-up suit and matching slippers, a casserole in her hands.

"You had me pretty worried," Frances said while walking to the kitchen and setting the casserole down on the table. "I made chicken soup for you yesterday. I came up. I called. I made enough noise to wake up the dead. Where were you?"

"I'm sorry. I took a pill that really knocked me out. I didn't hear a thing."

"Well, I worry about you."

"You're a very thoughtful person, Mrs. G., and I love you for it."

"Thanks for the chicken soup. I promise to have some of it later, but right now I have to go to work." Allison put an arm around Mrs. G. and walked her to the door again. "Ah...CHOO! I've already missed half a day," she said through newly stuffed nostrils.

"Bless you. You shouldn't be going anywhere with that cold," Mrs. G. pointed out gently. "But if you must, at least change your clothes. Weren't you wearing that outfit yesterday afternoon?"

Allison looked down. Her black pants were wrinkled, and her sweater was no longer tucked into them. She smiled. "Yes. I guess I should change. Thanks again." She closed the door and took to the bathroom.

Brushing her long brown hair into a barrette, she applied liquid make-up under her eyes. And they call this stuff *concealer*, she thought while frowning into her reflection. The only thing it concealed was the fact that it was overpriced. She frowned again. It didn't matter what she looked like. What mattered was how she was going to explain her "journey" once she got to the ChemProbe lab.

CHAPTER FIVE

"You should have stayed home today. A cold is not good for public relations," Robin Page teased. He and Horace Banks had been at the lab since the night before, working to perfect the new capsule. "You look awful," he emphasized.

Allison ignored his comment and walked over to Zelda's cage. She poked in a finger, and the chimp sluggishly tugged on it.

"Zelda doesn't appear to be getting any better," she said, her mouth making kissing sounds to the once playful chimp.

"We're working on an extension of the original capsule," Horace Banks offered while accurately measuring a blue liquid into a test tube and giving it a little shake. "Did you bring the sample we used for the media presentation?" He poured the liquid into another clear tube and set it down into a tray.

"I don't have it," she said, her attention still on Zelda.

"Have you misplaced it'?" It was Robin Page who posed the question. "Or did you lose it all together?"

Allison turned away from the cage and faced them squarely. "I took it," she said softly.

Horace Banks looked up from his test tubes, his wire-rimmed glasses slipping to the end of his nose as his head jerked up. "Sounded like you said you took it, but that couldn't be right, could it?"

Robin Page began to laugh. "She's joking, Horace."

Taking a banana from a bowl, Allison sat down at the small metal table beside Zelda's cage and waved it at the limp chimp. "I'm not joking. I've had a really bad cold that I can't shake, so I took the capsule."

"I refuse to believe you would consider doing such a thing, Allison," Horace Banks said with irritation. "It was sheer lunacy on your part to even contemplate taking the capsule without authorization or even supervision."

"I know…and I'm sorry."

"How could you be so irresponsible'?" Robin reprimanded. "The capsule isn't ready to be tested on humans, and you know it!"

"I know. I apologized. What more can I—"

"Wait." Horace Banks put up a hand to silence them. "Anger isn't going to get us anywhere." He picked his medical bag up from one of the counters and sat his rotund body down across from Allison. "The capsule was tested on a human, and that human is still alive. We'd be better served to ask relevant questions of Allison." He removed a thermometer from the bag. "Stick out your tongue." He checked the pallor of her skin and shook the thermometer.

"Open." He peered into her mouth. "And close," he said, tapping her chin up to close her mouth. Taking up her wrist, he kept time with his watch.

With her cooperation, the doctors had her change into a hospital smock, open in the back, which Allison detested, and began a thorough examination. She stared into the tiny light and followed it according to the instruction of Dr. Banks. Robin tested her reflexes. Her temperature was ninety-nine, not alarming; her reflexes slightly slower than normal; and her heart beat, though a bit rapid, was reasonable under the circumstances. Satisfied, the three sat around the table, Horace insisting she drink plenty of water, which she did with gusto.

"I need to know every detail," he said, pressing down the "record" button on a cassette player. He spoke his name, the names of those present, the location of the interview, and the date. "What happened after you took the twenty-four-hour capsule, Allison?" The lines in his face were deep, and if Allison didn't know better, his hair looked grayer than yesterday, the jowls in his face more defined.

"I went to the pharmacist with the prescription Robin gave me, and I had every intention of filling it."

Horace dragged his chair closer to her. "Well, you still have a cold, I see." He pushed over a box of tissues. "The time capsule did not cure your cold, so it is a failure." He shook his head in dismay.

"On the contrary."

"What do you mean?" Robin snapped impatiently. "You still have your cold, so the capsule doesn't work."

"Well, that depends."

"On what?" Robin sat back into his chair and folded his arms across his chest.

"It depends on your definition of success and failure." Allison smiled neatly. "This capsule is time release in that it releases time! Last night I traveled back to the year 1969, which is *twenty-four years*, not hours, from our year of 1992."

The two men stared at her.

Allison related the particulars of her "journey" and the fact that her cold was no longer in evidence while in that year. She described the rooms as well as the four occupants. What she did not reveal was that she had not come back alone, that the love beads had accompanied her.

"I would say that was success."

"Oh my God, do you hear yourself?" Robin Page leaped up in his chair and ran his fingers through his hair in frustration. "Time travel? A twenty-four-hour cold capsule suddenly becomes a twenty-four-*year* time travel capsule?"

"Well, I've heard enough." It was Horace who hit the "stop" button on the recorder.

"Obviously the capsule induced a very vivid and lucid dream, and in that dream your cold was cured. Wouldn't you agree, Horace?" Robin turned to Dr. Banks for confirmation.

Horace Banks nodded. "I'm sorry, Allison. From what you've told us, I have to concur with Dr. Page." He got up and paced around the lab, the coattails of his white smock flying behind him.

"The capsule did nothing more than cause you to dream," he continued, "though hallucinate may be a more accurate term."

"NO! It was real," Allison objected.

Dr. Banks patted her hand. "For you it was, Allison, and if this is what happens when the capsule is taken, then Zelda must be experiencing some very disturbing dreams." The intercom interrupted him, and he reached over to pick up the phone. He spoke quickly and hung up. "The ChemProbe meeting has begun, Dr. Page. They are waiting for us in the conference room."

Robin bent down and took Allison's hand, patting it in the same patronizing manner as Horace Banks. "Go home and get some rest." They both turned and hastily left the lab.

Allison changed back into her street clothes and pulled her jacket from the back of one of the chairs next to Horace's test tubes. Bending over, she scanned the labels in search of the new forty-eight-hour capsules. Picking up a tube, she regarded it thoughtfully.

Forty-eight hours. Forty-eight years? I wonder.

Emptying the pill into the palm of her hand, she wrapped it in a tissue, crammed it into her pocket, and with a zip of her jacket, she left the building.

Allison walked around her neighborhood in a pensive daze as she agonized over the guilt of having stolen the capsule. It was wrong. Good girls didn't do such things. But she had done it, hadn't she? She had done it to prove something the doctors at ChemProbe refused to believe: that she had gone back in time. And with the forty-eight-hour capsule, she planned to do so again.

Before going up to her apartment, she knocked on Frances Giovani's door and was immediately invited in.

"Come with me, child, you look worse than you did when you left here." Allison followed Frances into the kitchen, and the woman headed straight to the refrigerator and filled a tall glass with orange juice. "Drink this. You need plenty of liquids."

"I don't know what I need anymore," Allison replied, sipping the juice. She placed the glass down on the coffee table and looked around the living room. "It's so homey down here," she commented warmly, eyes glancing over the framed photos on top of the television set. "Your family surrounds you even though they're not here."

"But they were here, dear. At one time my entire family lived in this building."

"I don't understand."

"The brownstone was once a single family home. When the market crashed in 1929, the family lost a great deal of money and had to rent the rooms as units to make ends meet." She picked up one of the framed photographs and sat down beside Allison. "This is my son Marco."

Allison's eyes widened, and her smile froze. The young man in the picture wore his hair in a long ponytail that cascaded down his back.

"That's my son. Don't let the long hair fool you. This picture was taken around 1969, I think. He was living here while going to college. He's married now…to the girl on the right."

"Where?" Marco's arm was around the girl and he was smiling. Allison recognized Doe-eyes immediately. "Which apartment?"

"Your apartment. He chose the third floor to avoid parental interference." She shook her head. "He was such a rebellious young man back then. I'm so relieved now that he's settled down and has a family of his own."

Allison grew paler. "I have to go," she said, rising abruptly.

"Yes, of course." Mrs. G. returned the photo to the top of the television set. "You need your rest, and here I am rambling on about the past. I'm sorry."

"I just can't seem to concentrate on anything but this blasted cold. I don't mean to be short."

"I understand, Allison." Mrs. G. walked to the door. "When you're feeling better, we can spend some time together."

Up in her apartment, Allison changed into a pair of flannel pajamas and, nursing a cup of tea, sat in the wicker rocker by the bedroom window.

"Her son—Marco—and Doe-eyes were both in that picture, and I didn't even know they existed until I took the twenty-four-hour capsule."

It wasn't a dream!

She rocked back and forth and began to cry, frustrated tears streaming down her face in torrents. "It wasn't a dream," she repeated. "It wasn't a dream." She set her teacup on the window ledge and beside it, the crumpled tissue with the forty-eight-hour capsule.

I have to know.

Steadily rocking, Allison picked up the cup, brought the capsule to her lips once again…and swallowed.

CHAPTER SIX

"Make it stop!" she breathed in panic. "Please, God, make it stop!" The loud, shrieking siren shattered the silence in the room, and her hands flew up to cover her ears. The rocker was gone, and Allison was sitting on the bedroom floor by the window, afraid to open her eyes. She did so slowly, and her hazy vision met blackness, the blackness of the window. Fighting to focus, she struggled to get up, lost her footing, and hit her head against the windowsill.

Of course! Forty-eight years ago. World War II!

If it's not one war, it's another, she thought, recalling 1969 and Vietnam. She stared at the blackout shade and slackly rose to her wobbly feet, her right hand rubbing the rising bump on the back of her head. It was several minutes before her eyes drew on any light in the room. First flashes, then a dim glow, until her eyes accepted her new surroundings.

Nothing was familiar this time…nothing at all.

Standing upright, she sighed evenly as the air raid siren died down, her weight supported against a dresser of fine cherry wood. The wind-up clock on top of a lacy scarf confirmed the time. Ten o'clock. Next to the clock was a crystal tray with a brush, mirror, and perfume atomizer. Beside the perfume were a jewelry box and a framed photograph of a young man in uniform, a handsome sailor with dark, wavy hair. She stared a moment at the familiar blue eyes and bright smile. Lightly, she touched a hand to his face before moving away from the dresser and to the partially open bedroom door.

The back of a woman came into view, hands clutching the black receiver of a telephone. "When will this be over? I miss him so much," the woman sobbed.

The blow to Allison's head had spawned a headache, creating havoc with her vision. Reason still prevailed, and she deduced that since no one could see or hear her in 1969, so it was safe to assume the same to be true in 1944, where she believed she was. She walked confidently into the living room just as the woman hung up the telephone. The woman turned in alarm, a hand flying to her mouth. "Who are you, and how did you get into my home?"

"You can see me?"

"How did you get in here?" she repeated. "And in pajamas!"

"I'm not sure." Allison rubbed her sore head and blinked several times. The woman was pregnant. She was also very familiar. "Fire escape...I think."

No, it couldn't be!

"Mrs. Giovani?" she asked, staring at the youthful Mrs. G., whose hair was dark with tiny pin curls framing her face, a flowered smock covering her protruding belly.

"Yes...but who are you?"

Allison thought about this for a moment, stymied as to how she could explain her sudden materialization.

"My name is Allison. I was trying to find my friend's place, and I guess I wandered into the wrong apartment building and hit my head when I heard the air raid siren. Your window was unlocked."

Further words failed her, and she stood in the living room of the apartment, pale and confused, as the bump on her head grew larger. Her eyes took a quick inventory: a dark-blue flowered studio couch sat against one beige wall, two end tables of walnut, a floor lamp behind a soft, comfortable matching blue chair. Ashtrays were carefully placed throughout the room.

"Wandering? Lights are out, and now we are in the middle of a drill!"

"I am so sorry—" she winced, touching a hand to the bump.

"Well—Ali—you don't mind me calling you that do you?"

"Not at all."

"It's after ten. I can't very well toss you out." She motioned for Allison to follow her to the kitchen and sit down at the square wooden table. "I'll put on a pot of coffee, and you can tell me what you do remember."

Allison's eyes trailed across the kitchen counter. A two-slice toaster, an orange juice squeezer, and a drip coffee pot.

So this is 1944?

"You were crying," she commented in an attempt to keep the conversation going.

"It's hard being pregnant with your man off to war." Frances placed two cups down on the table and sat across from Allison. "Do you live in the neighborhood?"

"I think so."

"Why did you ask if I could see you?"

"I...I don't know," Allison stammered.

"That's a nasty bump on your head. Let me get you some ice." She removed a few cubes from the freezer tray and wrapped them in a dishtowel. "Helps the swelling go down."

"Thank you." Allison held the cold cubes to the lump. "What year?"

"Excuse me?"

"What—"

"I heard you the first time. That must have been some hit you took. It's 1944 of course." Frances pulled a cigarette from the pack in front of her and lit it. "Cigarette?"

"I don't smoke. Should you be smoking? I mean… you're pregnant."

"What difference does that make?"

The telephone saved Allison from further explanation. She listened to Frances's account of the arrival of an "intruder," catching snatches of the conversation.

"No, it's okay. She hit her head and can't seem to remember much. She'll have to stay the night. No, I'm not worried. Says she got in through the window. Yes…okay. I'll check the windows in the future. See you in the morning."

Frances arranged the studio couch with blankets and a pillow. "Maybe after a good night's rest you'll remember something in the morning and can go home. You must have family worrying about you."

"Thank you, Mrs. Giovani." Allison drew the blankets up to her chin.

"Call me Frances."

"Good night, Frances." Allison closed her eyes, and the room faded once again into blackness as she drifted into a sound sleep.

CHAPTER SEVEN

Allison awoke to the aroma of bacon and very strong coffee. Though she still nursed a slight headache, all signs of her cold had vanished. She neatly folded the blankets and put them with the pillow at one end of the couch before joining Frances in the kitchen.

"Good morning, Ali." In a blue-flowered smock, Frances was busy at the stove, frying eggs and bacon in a wide pan. "I thought you might need a hearty breakfast." She carefully arranged the eggs, bacon, and toast on a large dish and placed it in front of Allison.

Allison looked solemnly down at the dish. "Cholesterol isn't good for the body. Besides, I'm a vegetarian."

"What in hell are you talking about? What's cholesterol?"

"Never mind." Allison brought the black coffee to her lips and took a sip, sorry she had said anything at all. She would have to tread softly if she wanted to fit into 1944 until the forty-eight hours were up. "I really have no appetite, but thank you for the breakfast."

"Food rationing means wasting no food." Frances dragged the dish toward her. "I'm eating for two, so I guess it couldn't hurt." She picked up the greasy bacon and chewed off a piece. "Do you remember anything?" she asked, lighting another cigarette, her third according to the evidence in the ashtray.

"Things are still a bit fuzzy."

"Well, after some thought, I decided you can stay here. It gets pretty lonely for me." She filled their cups again. "I can call my doctor—"

"No! I mean…I'm sure to remember more in a couple of days."

The back door leading to the kitchen opened, and a curvaceous woman entered in a tight purple dress, her hair rolled up in curlers. "So this is your intruder?" the woman asked, helping herself to a cup of coffee and taking the chair beside Allison.

"This is Ali. Ali, meet Lois." Frances introduced the two women, and Allison had the distinct impression that Lois was not fond of "the intruder."

Lois reached out red, perfectly manicured fingernails and touched Allison's left hand. "No wedding band. You really are alone, aren't you, honey?" She turned to Frances. "She's built like a brick shithouse. Should I be worried?"

Frances rolled her eyes upward and shook her head without answering.

"Are *you* married?" Allison asked, the second cup of coffee trying her nerves.

"Nah, but I'm holding my breath for Franny's brother, John, ain't that right, Franny?"

Frances frowned. "So you say."

Lois drained her cup in two gulps and pushed it in front of her. "No time for a refill. I just came by to check out the competition." She smiled down at Ali as she got up and aimed her finger like she was pointing a gun. "See ya, wouldn't wanna be ya." Out she walked, wiggling through the back door as quickly as she had wiggled in. Frances was still shaking her head.

"You didn't seem to care much for her comment about your brother," Allison remarked.

"Oh, she's a good kid, but Johnny deserves better."

"Is he the sailor you have framed on your dresser?"

"Sure is. My husband is in the army. His picture is beside my bed. You must have missed it." Frances looked up at the kitchen clock and hustled the dishes into the sink. "I've got ironing to do and errands to run, Ali."

Allison looked down at her pajamas. *I can't very well go out in this.*

"Then there's the Victory Garden to attend to out front." Hands on hips, she sized up Allison's appearance and bit her lower lip. "I think I can find something suitable for you to wear. Before my pregnancy, I was about your size."

"Maybe I'll remember something along the way." Allison smiled, intrigued by the idea of accompanying Frances around the city.

"We have to deliver some scrap to the heap for The Cause," Frances continued while rummaging through her closets. "We can even take in a little window shopping. It's been a long time since I did that." She picked out a red dress and handed it to Allison. "This one's sure to flatter the figure, though yours doesn't need much flattering, honey." She walked with quick steps over to the dresser. "I think I have a new bra you can wear." Allison took the bra and smiled as Frances tossed it over. "We'll have to do something with your hair. How do you usually wear it?"

Allison shrugged. "Down, I guess."

"You guess?" Frances slapped her hands to her thighs and smiled. "The woman doesn't even remember what she looked like! We'll just have to fix that." Fingers flying, Frances set about arranging Allison's hair in various upsweeps, bobby pins sticking into her head, making Allison wince with pain.

"I don't think this will work, Frances. The pins hurt."

"Okay, okay." Frances eyed her thoughtfully. "I think you would be such a perfect match for my Johnny! Wait until you meet him! And Johnny likes the pageboy, and I think you'd be a smash fixed up that way. Mind if I cut your hair a couple of inches? It's too long to roll. The bangs work, that's for sure."

"Johnny? Cut my hair?"

She was in this time only a scant few hours, and she was already expected to change for a man? She had read a lot about the swiftness of wartime romance and grew fidgety with what Frances apparently had in mind.

In the kitchen now, Frances spread some newspaper on the floor and took scissors to Allison's waist-length locks, snipping off almost three inches before parting it over to the side. She plugged in a curling iron and began to roll Allison's hair under.

"Johnny is on forty-eight-hour leave and due here tonight. I just know he's going to fall for you like a ton of bricks, Ali!" She took various shades of lipstick and rouge from an over-sized make-up case and applied it with experience. "There!" She held a hand mirror up to Allison. "You like?"

Allison smiled at her reflection. "I like."

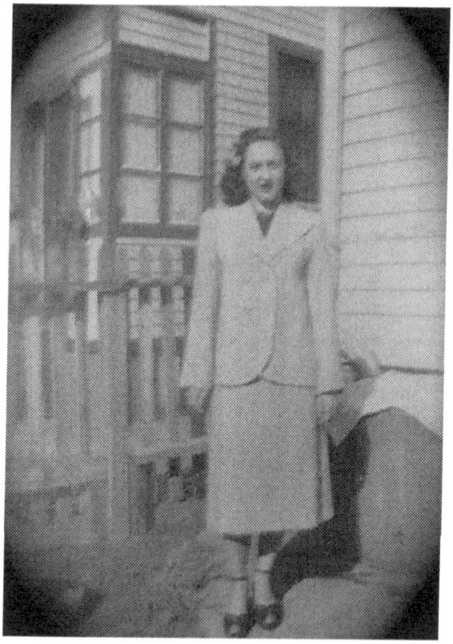

CHAPTER EIGHT

New York City in 1944 wasn't what Allison McKay expected. She wished she'd paid more attention in history class back in high school. So much had changed over the years that she kept biting her tongue, almost saying, "Hey, the World Trade Center is going to be right there," then catching herself just in time. Returning to the brownstone would be a welcome relief.

"Hang on a sec." Frances tugged Allison by the sleeve of her coat and dragged her over to a store window. "I love to look in jewelry stores, and Tesla timepieces are always so unique. These people specialize in watches, and the detail and craftsmanship is beautiful. They are inspired by everything around them. Look."

Allison stood beside Frances and cupped her two hands up to the window to peer in. There were watches lined up on tiny satiny pillows and others displayed on jewelry trees and atop their boxes. They were unique and expensive because they were painstakingly handcrafted and fashioned to make everyday objects into jeweled-encrusted timepieces. Any gemstones used in the settings were of the highest-grade rubies, diamonds, sapphires, and emeralds available to that market. From what Frances said, owning a Tesla timepiece was on par with owning Tiffany jewelry. In fact, both companies sprang up around the same time, but Tesla remained true to only carrying watches.

And what watches they are! Allison spied a piece that looked like a small gold Easter basket. The "eggs" were sapphires and rubies, and one of them cleverly displayed the face of the watch. Another watch was a replica of a grandfather clock. Each number on the dial of the face of the watch was made of tiny diamonds. Still another was a watch worn as a ring.

"Look at that one," Frances was saying. "That must be for a mother-to-be." She pointed to a stork carrying the baby in a bundle. The baby's face was the face of the watch, and it was bundled in a "blanket" of pink diamonds, clearly a gift for a baby girl. "I would never want something like that," she was quick to add. "I'm kind of superstitious. I'd have to wait until long after the baby was born, and then it wouldn't be the same."

"Why's that?"

"We don't know if the baby is a boy or a girl, Ali, though I've a feeling I'm having a boy."

Allison nodded. *Go with that, Frances, and you'd be right.*

"Couldn't hurt to go in." Frances motioned to the door.

Allison smiled. "Couldn't hurt."

They rang the bell, and the proprietor buzzed them inside. The store was small but brightly lit and clean of clutter. Each timepiece was displayed in the same manner as the storefront window. The sparkle was dazzling, and Allison was immediately drawn to a small case containing several watches on gold necklace chains. In the center of the hanging watches was a lapel watch pin made of diamonds and white gold. The face of the watch was square and pink and around it the diamonds formed several leaves.

"A lapel watch!"

The proprietor bent over the case to unlock its contents.

"Would you like to see it?" He moved the sliding doors aside and set the watch out onto a black velvet cloth. "This is additionally unique in that it is worn on the lapel with a pin clasp that is very strong and sturdy." He smiled in the hopes that this encouraged a sale.

"That sure is beautiful, Ali." Frances commented.

Together they bent down and looked at the watch. The numbers were clear and sharp and so were the diamonds. "It really is. Maybe one day…"

The proprietor snatched the watch and put it back in its case. "Will there be anything else?" he remarked tightly.

"No." It was Frances who answered. "Thanks."

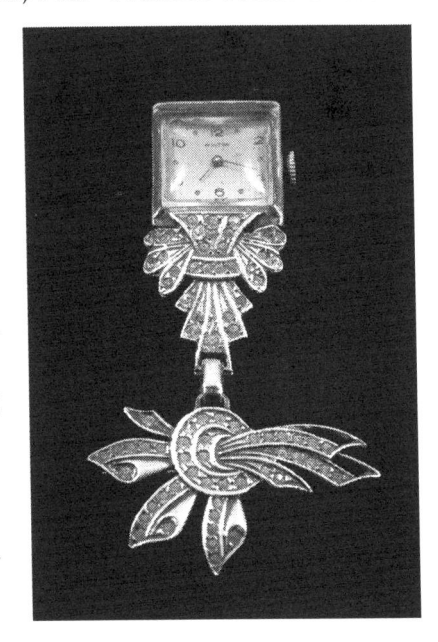

They continued up the busy street and Allison was grateful to be out in the fresh air despite how much cleaner and different it felt from her time.

"We have one more stop, and it's an important one."

"Important how?" Allison asked while keeping quick steps beside her. "Are you holding out on me?"

Frances laughed. "Oh dear, no! But it's not only our country in crisis, but also women are having a beauty crisis as a result. The most important asset we have is our gams. They literally carry us through life, Ali. If you want to keep your man, you have to have good gams!"

"Oh my God, are you serious?" Allison laughed louder.

"That's my belief, and I'm stickin' to it." Frances paused in front of a storefront with a red, white, and blue awning. "We're here."

Allison was still wondering how they were going to get these good gams when she looked up at the glass storefront sign—The Emporium—and followed Frances, who made a beeline for a booth called the Leg Make Up Bar. Allison knew a little about the art of stocking painting during wartime. "I just never knew I'd be experiencing it," she mumbled to herself while staring at the variety of jars and bottles in front of her.

Frances turned, a bottle in her hand. "Did you say something, Ali?"

"Talking to myself."

"Well, Hedda Hopper says that is a sign of intelligence, and she's a columnist for Hollywood, so talk away, dear!" She turned back to the counter and motioned for assistance.

Allison stepped up alongside Frances at the counter. Two women were in uniforms of matching, very short, puffy skirts and frilly white short-sleeve blouses. Their hair and make-up were identical, and Frances said that in many cases twins worked at these booths. Allison learned these women were known as "leg models" and were responsible for demonstrating the painting of the product to encourage consumer sales.

"Isn't it just terrible what has happened to women's stockings since the war?" Frances was saying.

"I guess so," Allison stumbled. "I really don't remember!" *Thank God for amnesia, real or imagined!*

Frances exchanged a few pleasantries with the ladies and then lined up different canisters and jars in front of them from the display stand. "I prefer the lotions and the creams. The liquids drip too much. We're doing our part by giving up our nylons, and this is the way to feel better about our sacrifice, Ali."

Ali picked up an amber bottle and read the label: Vanishing Crème. *Don't need any of this. I'll be vanishing soon enough.*

"The cosmetic stocking make-up that I look for usually has color and texture, just like real legs, else there is no reason for it," Frances continued. "Make-up hosiery has to go on evenly without streaks, though you can certainly draw an artful line for a seam," she added. "And it should have quick-drying properties and not stick to the skin or rub off. We also have to make sure that it has a little talc in it, because that can add sheen for realism."

"A lot to remember."

"But easy to apply, and you will thank me!"

The sales staff set them up with a short supply of leg make-up and put it all in a lovely lavender shopping bag, along with a free bottle of clear nail polish, which stymied Allison.

"Serves a dual purpose, Ali. You can use it for your nails, or you can repair rips or runs in the precious real stockings that you probably own." She bit her lip. "Sorry, I forget that you don't know where you belong, so you probably don't even know what you own."

"Don't apologize." Allison shifted the little shopping bag into her other hand and looped the free one through Frances's arm, something she imagined a woman of that time would do with friends. "And thank you for setting me up with what I may need."

They continued back in the direction of the brownstone, grateful the weather wasn't too cold, both of them separately thinking about the lapel watch.

"That would have looked great on you, Ali," remarked Frances when they finally arrived at the brownstone stoop.

Allison smiled and shrugged as she followed Frances up to her apartment on the third floor.

"Fix your face while I fix supper," Frances said on her way into the kitchen. Allison brightened. The excitement of her journey had depleted her appetite. Aside from coffee (and a hot cross bun at the corner deli), her stomach was empty. If Frances was as good a cook in 1944 as she was in 1992, Allison was in for a treat.

"What are we having?" Allison couldn't help asking.

"Johnny's favorite: spaghetti and meatballs with homemade tomato sauce." Frances turned on the radio in the kitchen and happily sang along with the Andrews Sisters. Her slightly off-key voice was melodic, making Allison feel soothingly comfortable and very much at home. Until now, "home" was merely a place to sleep and eat. Work always came first, leaving very little time to turn a residence into a home. Her whole life had been a series of residences—stopovers to the next destination. There had been no solidity to her existence.

It was nearing seven, and Allison was setting the dining room table when the doorbell rang. Frances was filling a casserole at the time and called from the kitchen.

"Ali, get the door, will you? He's always forgetting his key!"

A knot formed in the pit of her stomach. What if he doesn't like me? she thought nervously. More importantly, what difference did it make?

The doorbell rang again, and she ran to the mirror in the foyer to check her new "look" before answering. *Okay, Ali, here goes nothing!* She swung open the door swiftly.   Leaning heavily against it, John Minetti nearly fell into the room. Allison backed away quickly, misjudged the height of her too-large, borrowed shoes and tripped backward. Johnny caught her around the waist and forcefully pulled her back up before she could fall.

"Well, what have we here!" he said smiling, his arms around her longer than necessary.

Frances rushed into the living room. "I see you two have met!"

Johnny untangled himself from Allison and hugged Frances warmly. "I can smell the tomato sauce, Franny, but the live tomato is an even tastier morsel!" He removed his cap at once and pecked Frances on the cheek. Allison rolled her eyes and smiled.

"Stop joshing, will you. This is Ali…a new friend I've met."

"Any friend of my sister's is a friend of mine. John Minetti," he said, extending his hand. His eyes glanced over the red dress, hesitating at each curve. They traced the black piping that sloped softly between her breasts, around her small waist, and down the side of her legs. The legs...Betty Grable should have such legs! He gave a long whistle.

"You from around here?"

Allison turned pleading eyes to Frances, who quickly came to the rescue.

"Ali hit her head. She wandered in through the bedroom window during a drill. We've been trying to jog her memory, but no dice so far."

John put an arm around the waist of each woman and escorted them into the dining room, all the while his attention on Allison. "Maybe I can do a little jogging while I'm here and roll the dice in my favor," he teased.

Frances' feast was everything Allison knew it would be. She ate slowly, allowing her stomach time to adjust. Her focus was no longer on the food but on John who kept her mesmerized with buddy stories and jokes he'd heard from shipmates.

"More vino?" he asked.

Allison nodded and watched his slender fingers fill her wine glass, his eyes never leaving hers. He was corny, but cute.

"What say we go out tonight? The Copa maybe?"

"The Copacabana?" Allison asked in clarification.

"The one and only," Johnny laughed and took a last swig from his glass. "Is there another?" he asked.

Allison shook her head, straining for some quip to answer him with.

"I'm not up for dancing in my condition," Frances said in a quick save that caused Allison an audible sigh, "but Ali might enjoy it."

Johnny patted his sister's belly. "Right, the bun in the oven. Well, you're coming along anyway. I've missed you, Sis."

The thought of dancing in Frances's heels was frightening. She might manage a waltz, but jitterbugging would be out of the question, and Allison began to object. Johnny was having none of it.

"I'm on forty-eight-hour leave, and I plan on abusing every minute of it," he joked.

"No use arguing with him, Ali. Johnny's a stubborn one."

"I'm at your mercy then," Allison teased. "Who knows where we'll be in forty-eight hours."

"I like this girl, Sis!"

CHAPTER NINE

Allison had to admit that the most she knew about the historic Copacabana nightclub was from the Barry Manilow song by the same name. She had read about the famous celebrities who played there during the war, and the fiasco that occurred in 1944 when singer and then serviceman Harry Belafonte was turned away and denied admission because he was black. She also knew the mob had ties to the club, but that was the extent of her knowledge. Truth be told, she didn't want to know more than that.

Allison scanned the room. The smoky dance floor of the Copa was crowded, and you could see the smoke move through the crowd and rise like the steam off hot-tarred pavement. The music was loud, and the place was jumping with bodies in a dancing frenzy. The only indication that there was a war on was the uniforms of sailors, soldiers, and marines clutching willful partners to Benny Goodman's "In The Mood." Johnny led them over to a small round table in front of the stage. It was covered with a white tablecloth, and there was a small shaded lamp in the center. Johnny pulled out a chair for Ali, and then rounded to Frances to pull hers out before he sat down.

"You take my breath away, Ali." he took her hand and kissed it.

Chivalry is not dead in 1944, so what happened to change that in my time?

No sooner had the thought taken residence in her head than it was cast out quickly. In a tight, black evening dress, Frances's friend Lois wiggled over to their table and immediately sat on Johnny's lap, planting a long, passionate kiss on his lips.

"I've been waiting for you, Sailor," she cooed, rubbing her nose against his. "Even saved a spot on my dance card just for you." With a long, red nail, she wiped her lipstick from his lips and turned around to Allison. "Well, well, well, look at you all dolled up! Isn't that Franny's old dress?"

"Don't be rude," Frances reprimanded. "Ali is our guest."

Johnny gently pushed Lois off his lap. "Sorry, honey, but my dance card was filled hours ago." He got up from his chair and held a hand out to Allison. "Ali, dance with me?"

Allison smiled nervously as Johnny led her onto the dance floor.

Seething, Lois plopped down beside Frances. "Well, if that don't beat all," she huffed. "She's got a helluva nerve showing up here. Why'd she have to pick your window to crawl into?"

Frances laughed, taking shameful delight in her friend's disappointment. "Shut up, Lois," she said, her eyes following John and Ali.

The band started up again as a young brunette took center stage and began to sing, her velvety voice slowly stringing the words together in one long sultry note.

"Gonna take...a Sentimental Journey."

With smooth steps, Johnny held Allison closely to him, and they glided across the dance floor as if they'd been doing so for years.

"You're a knock-out in that dress, you know." With a hand he lifted her chin to meet his eyes.

Allison lowered her head again quickly and blushed. "But not a very good dancer."

"In my arms you're Ginger Rogers. Fred Astaire would be jealous." He pressed his cheek to hers and drew her to him. Allison could have sworn she heard herself swoon.

They danced to every waltz, and Allison heaved a sigh of relief at having been spared the jitterbug. On more than one occasion, another soldier, sailor, or marine tried to cut in, but Johnny gently shooed each away with, "Sorry fellas, she's with me."

It was one o'clock in the morning when they finally arrived back home. Frances went to bed, leaving them sitting on the front steps of the brownstone, Johnny silently smoking a cigarette while Allison kicked off her shoes and rubbed her tired feet. The November night was cold, and Johnny put an arm around her shoulders and flicked the cigarette into the street.

"See that car," he said, pointing to a blue Chevy. "The one on the blocks?"

"Yes."

"I had every intention of fixing it and getting it back on the road. Then the Japs interfered, and my project will have to take a back seat to the war." He took her white-gloved hand and brought it to his lips, clouds of cold air swirling from his mouth as he spoke. "The car, even the war, means very little since I met you."

"Oh, Johnny…I…"

"Be right back!" Johnny ran up the brownstone steps and disappeared inside the house and returned with a camera. "Come on, let me see how great this car is gonna fit you, baby." He got up, and she followed him to the curb. "Up!"

Before she could protest, his arms were around her waist, and he effortlessly picked her up and positioned her on the hood of the car.

"Shh." He faced her and put his finger to her lips to silence her. "I want a picture of you smiling." He placed a hand on either side of her and looked into her eyes. For a long moment neither of them moved. Finally, as if to both break a spell, Johnny kissed her and said, "Indulge me, Ali. I'm on a forty-eight-hour leave."

"Me, too," she whispered softly against his mouth.

"What?" He laughed. "You really are a mystery woman! You say the darndest things."

But it's true, Allison thought. Yet I have no desire to leave.

This time and these people had worked a path into her heart and she wanted to know more. She felt a deep need to see what was ahead.

"Say cheese, baby." Johnny took a step back and snapped a few photos. "I'm going to keep this one," he teased.

Johnny straightened up and with his free hand turned her face to meet his. "Where have you been all my life?"

In 1992, she wanted to say, but kept silent, a smile on her lips at what in 1944 was probably considered to be an amorous and very serious question. Looking into his blue eyes, she tried to concentrate on his handsome face—the long angular jaw, the tiny scar just below his right eye, his thick, full lips. She began to wonder when it would happen, when she would disappear completely. More importantly, how it would affect his life. Deep inside, where she never allowed anyone else to venture, she found she desperately wanted to stay right where she was, in 1944 and in John Minetti's arms. He saw the look on her face and tenderly kissed her. This time Allison heard herself swoon. So did Johnny.

"Honey, forty-eight hours isn't a very long time to get to know someone," he said, breaking the kiss.

How right he is, Allison thought. This time it was she who silenced him, boldly brushing her lips against his. If only there was a way to remain here, a way to keep this happy moment.

CHAPTER TEN

Johnny had graciously let Allison sleep in his bed while he slept on the couch. Up early the next morning, Allison was disappointed to find Johnny gone, the couch clear of pillows and blankets. She immediately headed for the kitchen where Frances sat, a cup of coffee in front of her and a cigarette smoldering in the ashtray.

"Don't worry, Ali, he'll be back." She poured Allison a cup from the pot she kept on a hot plate in the center of the table. "He went out early. Didn't say why, but I have my suspicions." There was a smile on her face that relieved Allison. "Swapping spit last night on the porch, eh?" she teased.

"It's that obvious?"

Frances nodded. "I had a feeling you might be the one for Johnny. Call it women's intuition, but I feel certain that you, Ali, are the woman he's been searching for. Just hang in there, honey."

The expression on Allison's face was one of sadness. In a little less than twenty-four hours, she'd be gone, and there wasn't a damn thing she could do about it.

"Why the frown?"

"I'm just worried, that's all." Allison refilled her cup and set the pot down on the hot plate. "I really like Johnny, but I'm afraid to…remember," she said carefully.

"That's a strange thing to say. Don't you want to remember?" Frances asked while lighting another cigarette.

Allison brought the cup to her lips and blew into it. "I just wish we had more time."

"Time is the enemy when there's a war on. But I have faith, Ali, and so should you." She pushed her pack of cigarettes over to Allison. "Go ahead, indulge. A good puff always settles my nerves. It might do the same for you."

Though she knew it wouldn't and was positive she shouldn't, Allison drew a cigarette from the pack and lit it just as Johnny came through the back door.

"Good morning! How are the two most beautiful women in the world?" he asked while helping himself to a cup of coffee, then bending down to peck his sister's cheek before sitting next to Allison and planting a quick kiss on her lips. "I have big plans for us today, Ali."

"What kind of plans?" she asked, tightening the belt around her borrowed chenille robe.

"I got my orders, and we're shipping out a little earlier than expected."

"When?" It was Frances who fretfully posed the question.

"This evening. So, if it's okay with you, Sis, I'd like to take in a movie with Ali today and spend the rest of my leave at home with the two of you."

"Of course it's okay," Frances replied. She stamped out her cigarette.

Allison stamped out her own cigarette and quickly lit another. *What if Johnny didn't come back alive? What if – .* The second cigarette made her as dizzy as the first, and she regretted ever picking one up in the first place.

"It's okay, baby," Johnny was saying. "We still have today and most of the evening."

"I have nothing to wear," Allison said impatiently. It was all happening too fast. She needed more time, but she was at the mercy of time, totally powerless while held in its grasp.

Frances cast a troubled look to Johnny. "Ali's family must be so worried about her," she fretted. "We had a talk about it this morning."

"Yeah, that's a problem. But I hoped our being together might shed some light for Ali. Landmarks, streets, anything could trigger something familiar. Don't you agree, Ali?"

"Maybe," she answered. What could she say? You're way off base? I know who I am; I just don't want to go home?

"Come with me, Ali," Frances said, getting up from the table. "I've got more dresses where we found the red one."

Wearing a simple blue dress and short white gloves, Allison and Johnny went to the theater to see *You Were Never Lovelier*, a Fred Astaire movie Allison had seen at least a hundred times. With Johnny beside her in the back of the theater, it was like she had never seen it before. Sharing a box of licorice, they kissed and cuddled, the movie a background to their wordless communication.

After the movie they walked the New York City streets, Allison's arm tucked through Johnny's, Frances's fur coat keeping her warm against the November cold. Her minutes in 1944 were ticking away. She would just have to make the best of the time she did have. It certainly wasn't going to happen now, not yet. Resigning herself to this fact brought some relief, and she tightened her hold on Johnny's arm.

"Remembering something?" he asked hopefully.

"In a way, not significant though." They stopped in front of the Tesla timepiece window and she peered in, again cupping both hands to the glass. "There was a gorgeous watch here, Johnny. It was a lapel watch. Frances and I saw it on our walk. I've never seen anything quite like it before." She scanned the window, but the lapel watch was gone.

Johnny pressed his hands to the window and smiled. "Nice ice." He straightened up, took her hand, and they continued their walk. "Lapel watch, eh?"

"Yes, it was right there in the center of the window."

"Newest rage, Ali, probably sold out fast."

She nodded and frowned. *Time doesn't matter, so why should I even wear a watch?*

And then a flash went off, and her attention moved away from the window and to the light and sound.

A roving photographer passed them as they came upon a quaint café on the corner and captured the moment.

"Such a beautiful couple. Please come inside to the restaurant, and I will develop your photograph."

He didn't wait for their answer as he hustled inside, Ali and Johnny quick on his heels.

"This okay with you?" he asked taking her hand.

Allison nodded.

They were escorted to a small table with a checkered cloth. Allison slid into the chair Johnny pulled out for her, and he put some change into the jukebox before sitting down. The arm of the machine slipped out a record and set it down on the turntable. "Sentimental Journey" sweetly filled the café. Allison smiled as Johnny reached his hand across the table to hers.

"Ali, you know I like you a lot, don't you?" he asked seriously.

"Do you?"

He tightened his hands around hers. "I know we haven't known each other long, but if given a chance, we could be good together."

"Johnny—"

A waiter came to the table and set down two coffees.

"There's a war going on and, well, I've never felt for any other woman the way I feel about you. I'd hate to lose the chance to get to know you."

"Johnny, I don't even know myself, remember?"

He reached into his pocket, pulled out a small square box, and placed it in the center of the table. "Ali, I'd like you to wait for me."

Allison looked down at the box and then up into his eyes. It would be so cruel to lead him on, to make a promise she may never be able to keep.

"Ali?"

"Johnny, you don't understand." She pushed the box toward him.

He pushed it back. "You think there may be someone else? Someone you don't remember?"

Allison sighed.

"Well, I don't care. I'll fight him for you." He pushed the box closer to her. "Will you at least see what it is before you give it back? It is very special, and I dumped a lot of dough on it," he said with a hurtful look.

Dough? He uses the word dough. How can I possibly be angry with a guy who uses the word dough?

Allison smiled sadly, lifted the lid, and stared into the box, immediately overwhelmed by the contents. The diamond lapel watch pin with the square pink face stared up at her, the tiny diamonds scattering into a leaf at its stem. She gasped as a lump formed in her throat, her eyes quickly filling up with tears.

"Oh, Johnny…the lapel watch…it's beautiful!" But there was no excitement in her voice, only melancholy. "I don't know what to say." She looked up at him. "Except that you have good taste," she added in a vain attempt at humor. "I now also know where you ran off to this morning and why the lapel watch was missing from Tesla's display window!"

"Say you'll wait." He took the watch and pinned it to the collar of the blue dress. "It's set for the right time," he added hopefully.

"You sure about that?" she mumbled.

"What?"

"Nothing." Allison lifted the watch and easily read the face. *Six o'clock.* What could she tell him? Sorry, Johnny, but I'm from the year 1992. You see, I took this cold capsule and went back in time to 1944. I may look twenty-five, but I won't be born until 1967 and—

Before she could complete her thought, the photographer returned, this time accompanied by a tall thin woman who Allison found hard to attach an age to.

Thirty, maybe? She was dark and beautiful in a very aristocratic way. Allison found herself torn with wanting to know more about her and wanting to run as far away from the woman as possible.

"My aunt needs no introduction. Allow her to sit at your table to discuss your future."

Johnny and Ali looked at each other and then to the woman. Her nephew looked to be still in his teens and wore a crumpled suit without a tie and was obviously making ends meet with his camera. But Allison was not sure what his aunt's story was, and she was going to be leery and wary. The woman wore a sleek black dress that shimmered when she walked, black patent leather heels, and on her head, holding back dark curly hair, was a large black hat. A white and lavender corsage covered the entire left side of her chest, a bracelet of crystals and pearls with matching earrings completing the outfit.

"I hope my nephew didn't scare you. He tends toward the dramatic because of my gift." She motioned to the empty chair at their table. "May I?"

"Sure." Johnny quickly rose to pull out her chair. "You a gypsy or something?"

She handed her card to Allison, but directed her words to Johnny. "I am a psychic medium. I help people with their spiritual course and investigate the best ways to reach their destination."

"Sounds like a lot of double talk to me," Johnny said.

Allison gave him a playful punch and looked down at the name on the card.

"Nina Davenport," she read aloud. "Why did you want to speak to us, Ms. Davenport?" She started to hand the card back.

"Please, keep it." She paused. "I come gifted, and I have insight to offer you on your destination." She looked pointedly at Allison and began to slowly peel off her gloves to reveal a multitude of rings of various stones and sizes adorning her fingers. Diamonds, amethyst, ruby, garnet, and around her neck, pearls, all dazzled in a distracting array of colorful light. "Your hand, please."

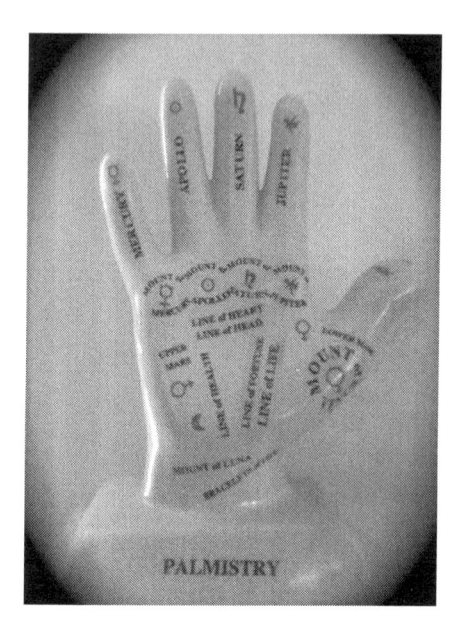

Allison looked directly into the woman's eyes. "Sure. I love this stuff." She stuck out her hand, palm up, into Nina Davenport's face. "Go ahead."

"Your palm is the map that will dictate the road you will travel." She closed Allison's fingers and held them tight. "The duality will soon change. Travel light."

Allison pulled her hand back. "So what the heck does that mean?"

Johnny was laughing. "I tell you, babe, it's like I always say, your guess is as good as mine."

Nina Davenport rose from the table and picked up her gloves. "Remember what I tell you now. Travel light." She offered a reassuring smile. "God bless you both on your journey."

Allison and Johnny were still watching her walk away when her nephew returned.

"That'll be two bucks, if that's okay with you folks," he said apologetically. "I'd give it to you for free for fighting the war, sailor, but a guy's got to eat." He put his head down and slid the photo over.

"Here's a fin, kid." Johnny folded the five-dollar bill into the kid's hand. "And never sell your work short."

"Thanks."

Johnny tucked the photo inside his shirt pocket.

"Johnny, let me see it," she pleaded.

"Nope. Not until you promise to wait for me, no matter what you remember while I'm gone." He leaned forward and kissed her. "Besides, I need this picture to remember you by."

"That's not fair. I don't have a picture of you."

He pulled out his wallet and took out a picture of himself in his uniform, called over to the waiter for a pen, and scrawled something on the back of it before handing it to her.

"You have to promise not to read it until after I've left," he said, handing it to her.

Allison sighed. "I promise." It was the same picture as the one on Frances' dresser. She smiled down at it before placing it carefully into the side pocket of her borrowed purse.

As intended, they spent the remainder of Johnny's leave at the brownstone with Frances. Both women were tearful when he left, Allison so inconsolable that Frances didn't know what to do to lift her spirits.

"I know it's hard, Ali, for you more so than for me. I know where my man is, but you don't even know your last name, or if you have someone in your life other than me and Johnny."

Allison choked back her tears with difficulty and blew into a tissue. "Ah...CHOO!"

"God bless you," Frances said, handing her a tissue.

The cold was returning, which meant Allison was that much closer to leaving 1944. She wiped her eyes and blew her nose into the tissue. The tears kept flowing.

"Come on, honey, it's girl time." Frances led her into the kitchen. "We can do facials and polish our nails! It's sure to pick up your morale." She bent down and placed a towel around Allison's neck. "We'll have a lot of fun. You'll see!" She turned and rummaged through the bottom drawer of the kitchen cabinet. "Now, where did I put that nail polish remover?"

In a pair of flannel pajamas, Allison was already applying the mudpack, her face a cakey brown, and Johnny's snapshot safely in her side pants pocket.

"Now, don't cry and don't smile. You mustn't move a muscle, or you'll crack the mudpack. I'll be right back."

"Where are you going?" Allison managed to say through the quick-setting facial. "To see if Lois has any nail polish remover."

Alone in the kitchen, Allison lifted the lapel watch to see the time. *I could disappear any time now.* She got up and headed for the living room for the pad and pencil by the telephone and returned to the kitchen quickly. She wrote "I remember home," sat back against the chair, and waited, praying it would happen while Frances was still with Lois. *What would Frances think if I vanished right here in front of her!* She felt the side pocket of her flannels for Johnny's picture and pulled it out. Johnny was gone and soon so would she. Flipping the picture over, she read the inscription.

"Ahh...CHOO!"

CHAPTER ELEVEN

November 23, 1992

Allison once again found herself on the floor, this time in her own kitchen.

This floor business is getting tiring.

The lapel watch traveled well, and she noted the time: one o'clock. She reached into the front pocket of her pajamas and took out Johnny's picture. I've got to know more about him, she thought. I've got to find out what happened—if he came back safely.

The telephone abruptly interrupted her thoughts. She let the answering machine pick it up and walked into the living room to listen to the caller.

"Allison, pick up the damn phone!" Robin Page's voice was clearly angry. "We know you stole one of the capsules from the lab. If you don't care about yourself, we do! And Zelda is another matter you have to know about. Allison, pick up!"

Reluctantly she picked up the phone, the mud pack cracking as she spoke. "Meet me at ChemProbe at seven tonight. Make sure Horace Banks is with you. I'll explain then." Allison hung up on a frustrated Robin Page.

She put the lapel watch beside the love beads in her dresser drawer and next to that, Johnny's picture. In the bathroom, she stared at her reflection in the mirror above the sink. Her face looked like a road map, the San Andreas Fault running down her left cheek, over her nose, and ending at her lips. She shook her head and laughed out loud. "What would Frances say?" Pressing a warm cloth to her face, she washed away the mudpack. She stepped into a black t-shirt and a fresh pair of jeans and spent the rest of the day combing the library for information on life in the 1940s.

In a nostalgia shop on Fifth Avenue, she purchased a few dresses and a small clutch purse. It was a little after five o'clock when she finally returned to the brownstone and found herself standing in front of Mrs. G.'s door. *Should she knock?* Would Frances remember? She decided to knock anyway and after several minutes, Mrs. G. answered, this time wearing a blue warm-up suit and slippers.

"Allison, how are you feeling?"

"Much better. May I come in?"

"Of course." Mrs. G. made tea for them and joined Allison in the living room. "I like the new hair cut, but was it wise, considering your cold I mean?"

"I did it myself," she lied. "I've been cooped up in the apartment for two days and needed a lift."

Frances nodded. "I know the feeling well, dear."

"Fr—Mrs. G., I'd like to ask you a few more questions about the brownstone, my apartment in particular."

"What would you like to know?"

"Who lived there during World War II?" She sipped her tea, careful to not meet Mrs. G.'s eyes.

"I did, with my husband Jerry and my brother Johnny. Those were tough times, I can tell you that. I was pregnant with Marco then."

"Wow. I find that fascinating! I was always interested in the women back then. Do you have pictures I could look at?"

Mrs. G. smiled. "I have an album full. Just a second." She got up and retrieved a thick photo album from a bookshelf and sat down beside Allison. "This one goes back the farthest—from when we were children." She opened the book. "This is me at age three…oh, and here's Johnny, he was six, I think."

Allison looked down at the two children. Mrs. G. had Shirley Temple locks, and Johnny's hair was cropped short. He was standing by a bicycle. As Mrs. G. turned each page, the life of the Minetti family unfolded before her. Frances had written neat captions at the start of each page, and soon they came to "The War Years," and there was Johnny's familiar Navy picture.

"Handsome young man," Allison noted with a smile.

"Still is, dear. He was twenty-six at the time and a shutterbug. He never went anywhere without his camera!"

While Mrs. G. turned to the next page, Allison quickly calculated his present age. Johnny would now be in his seventies.

On the next page, dead center was the picture of Allison and Johnny the young man had taken that day while they took their stroll in 1944.

So, he gave it to Frances! Why?

She and Mrs. G. looked down at the picture and then up at each other. "It's remarkable, isn't it? Her name was Allison, too, but we called her—"

"Ali."

"Why, yes, that's right."

"Did they ever marry?" Allison asked, feigning little interest.

Mrs. G. frowned. "She broke his heart—and mine, too, if the truth be known. She left quite abruptly and never came back, not even to let us know where she was living or how she was doing. We didn't even know her last name! Such a sweet girl," Mrs. G. commented wistfully. "It was all so long ago."

There was a long moment of silence between them.

Mrs. G. pointed to the pink-faced lapel watch. "Johnny bought that for her. It was an expensive gift for 1944, especially because it was a Tesla timepiece. To Johnny, it was a promise that she would wait for him. He was devastated when he came home for good and found she was gone."

"Was he okay? Did he come back without being hurt?"

"Minor wound was all." She pointed to another photo, Johnny's car on blocks in front of the house. "He finally managed to get that car on the road, but it remained immobile until around 1946, the spring, I think."

More pages were turned until they finally reached the present. John Minetti was still handsome with a full head of wavy white hair. But the sparkle was no longer in his eyes and there was tightness around his mouth.

"John practices law up in Westchester where he lives. Makes a good living…a shame he never married. He has no one to share his success with. Though he almost married a friend of mine. Lois was her name. But at the eleventh hour, he called everything off. He just never got over losing Ali."

Allison sighed, relieved a bit. "Such a sad story."

Mrs. G. patted her hand. "You know, dear, I rented you the apartment because you looked so much like her. I thought you were her daughter—that I'd find out what happened."

"Sorry."

"I've always made a point of steering Johnny away from here when I knew you were home. I've been doing so for four years now. I thought it would be so painful for him to…remember."

"I can understand why." Allison finished the tea. "When did he come home for good?"

"Christmas Eve 1944, on a medical discharge. Why?"

"Just curious." Allison looked up at the clock in the living room. Six thirty. "I have to go to work, Mrs. G., but thanks for the trip down memory lane. I enjoyed it."

"You work such strange hours."

Allison shrugged and smiled.

"Any time you feel like chatting, it's always my pleasure."

Before Allison left the brownstone for ChemProbe, she took the lapel watch and the photo from the dresser drawer. Now they would have to believe her.

CHAPTER TWELVE

Allison arrived at ChemProbe to find Zelda's cage empty. She shook her head, confident she knew what had happened.

"Zelda died last night," Dr. Banks confirmed as he entered the lab with Robin Page in tow.

"How many pills did you give her?" Allison asked while taking a seat at the metal table nearby. The doctors joined her.

"Two forty-eight-hour capsules," Robin answered sharply, still smarting from having been hung up on by Allison earlier in the day.

The realization that the chimp went back too far in one journey was easy for her to understand. The animal couldn't possible comprehend what was happening to her. But a human who was aware, that was another story, and the possibility of being able to return to 1944 lifted Allison's spirits.

"Where have you been?" Dr. Banks asked angrily. "If you were going to steal a capsule and insist on using yourself as a guinea pig, the least you could have done was to allow us to monitor you. I can't—"

"1944."

"What?" It was Robin who spoke.

"I've been in New York in the year 1944."

"That explains the hair," he said, pointing to her now limp pageboy, goading her into an argument.

Allison shot him an angry look.

"Well," Dr. Banks huffed, "obviously the capsule doesn't work. You've lost your mind, and we've lost Zelda."

"NO!" Allison objected. "Zelda went back too far. She couldn't know what was happening, and the shock of the transition between times must have killed her! But I understand and can deal with it…and I want to go back. I want to live in 1944." She leaned back against the cold metal chair. "The pill does work. My cold is gone."

With accuracy, Allison slowly revealed what had transpired the last two days. Most importantly, unlike the first journey, it was significant that she was seen and heard in 1944—actually able to participate in life in another time.

"I told you, the capsule releases time, and I am proof that it does just that."

"Your mind did it, Allison," Robin Page insisted, tapping a finger to his temple for emphasis. "Your mind."

Horace Banks concurred. "Allison, I believe that you believe you were in New York in 1944, but the idea that you were an active participant is inconceivable."

"As inconceivable as believing you can find a cure for the common cold?" she countered.

"If that is your comparison, yes," Dr. Banks agreed.

"I have proof."

The men looked at each other.

"What proof is that?" Robin asked gently, fearful that Allison had lost all hold on reality.

Allison took the lapel watch from the inside zipper of her purse. "Ever seen one of these before?"

Dr. Banks picked it up and examined it. "It's a beautiful antique, Allison, but surely that's all it is."

"You could have bought that yourself in one of the nostalgia shops in Manhattan," Robin pointed out.

"Give me a break! Like I could afford it on my salary."

"With installment payments you could." It was Robin's turn to examine the watch. "Forty or fifty years isn't old enough to qualify a purchase to bankrupt you."

Allison was beginning to feel she was wasting valuable time. *Time, time, time.* The word rolled over in her mind repeatedly. What would she do if they didn't believe her? In order for her to return, they would have to supply the capsules. Without the help of Page and Banks, the situation was hopeless. Then she remembered Johnny's picture and the personal inscription.

"Then explain this away, gentlemen." She pushed the photo of John Minetti across the table between them. "I met him, danced with him, and promised to wait for him. There is even a personal inscription on the back!"

"Nice looking," Dr. Banks commented.

"Okay looking," Robin said, the picture now in his hands. He turned it over and read the inscription. "How touching."

"Stop it!" She reached over and snatched the picture from his hands. "How dare you make light of this."

"Allison, didn't you just tell us that your landlady has a photograph of a girl resembling you? And didn't you inform us they referred to her as Ali?" She nodded. "Then it is likely that this picture belongs to that woman."

"That woman is me! What will it take for you to believe me?"

"I'm convinced this was all very cerebral, but certainly not physical, Allison." Robin was angry now. "You had two days to dream is what you had."

"Then explain the alleviation of my cold symptoms."

"You were overworked. You had that cold for a very long time. It's safe to assume plenty of rest did the trick."

Dr. Banks got up and paced a circle in front of them. "Let's examine this as if it really did happen—"

"It did!"

Horace stopped in mid-pace and put up a hand. "Hear me out, Allison. Just suppose it happened—that you could return to another time. To remain in that time you would have to have a supply of capsules for the remainder of your life. The effects cannot be guaranteed. You could even die prematurely. You would also know too much and inevitably you would try to change history."

"I thought I knew you, Horace," Robin interrupted. "I guess I was mistaken."

"You couldn't possibly survive," Dr. Banks continued, ignoring Robin's comment. He stopped and looked at Allison. "Then, of course, there is the aging process to consider."

"Come on, Horace, you're not buying this, are you?" Robin protested.

Horace Banks hesitation was enough for Robin Page.

"You are! I can't believe this! You, a scientific man, a doctor, is actually considering this tale of hers to be true?"

"There's a great deal we don't know, Dr. Page. I admit to being more than a little intrigued." He turned to Allison. "May I make a suggestion?"

"Depends on what it is," Allison answered guardedly.

"I want to arrange some physical tests, to make sure you are well after having taken the forty-eight-hour capsule. Afterward, I'd like you to see a colleague of mine."

"A psychiatrist, right?"

"Yes." He took a pad from inside his white lab coat and jotted down a name and number. "Make the appointment as soon as possible. I'll be sure to fill her in on my findings regarding the capsule."

Allison felt somewhat relieved. "Thank you, Dr. Banks."

Robin Page sighed heavily and ran his fingers through his thinning hair. "I don't believe you two, I really don't. What do you expect from your colleague, Horace, confirmation that Allison has gone nutso on us? Because that's what the verdict will be."

Allison shot up angrily from the chair. "For a man of medicine and science yourself, Dr. Page, you have a very closed mind."

"Yours is too open. You've been living alone too long!"

"How dare you!"

"I dare! I dare!" Robin shouted.

Horace Banks came between them. "How unprofessional of you both. Now stop this fighting at once, or I will be forced to toss you both out." He turned to Allison who had grabbed her purse and was heading for the door. "Make that call, Allison, and take all the necessary tests. I will decide what to do about this at that time."

Allison opened the door, her hand tightly on the knob. "It's November twenty-fourth. I'll give you full use of testing me for one month. When I return to 1944, and I promise you I will, you can both be witness to it. But it won't be in the lab. I have another place in mind."

"You've *lost* your mind!" Robin yelled.

"Why one month, Allison?" Horace asked.

"Because December twenty-fourth is when Johnny comes home, and I intend to be there when he does."

"When Johnny comes marching home again, hurrah, hurrah," Robin sang, mocking her.

"You're a jerk, Robin Page, and I hate you!" Allison slammed the door and left the ChemProbe building.

CHAPTER THIRTEEN

Over the next few weeks, Allison shuttled back and forth in a ChemProbe corporate limousine to Dr. Reva Mitchell's office on Park Avenue. She spent the mornings on the first floor where she donned a hospital smock for physical testing. The nurses monitored her heart and pulse rates and drew blood, two tubes a day. They picked, poked, and prodded her enough times to provoke the most patient of individuals. By noon she was always grateful to be back in her own clothes and in Dr. Mitchell's suite on the fifth floor.

Reva Mitchell was a comfortable person to be with—easy in her manner and totally open. She was never suspect in her approach to the idea of time travel. For Dr. Mitchell, Allison McKay might be that landmark case all doctors hope for, and Reva was thorough in guiding Allison with information regarding other explorations of time travel she had come across. Allison discovered that she was not alone—many people had gone back in time through hypnosis. Each day the doctor became more fascinated with Allison's story. Reva Mitchell believed the capsule induced an experience Allison was comfortable with and, much like a drug addict, wanted to maintain that state. Yet Allison McKay insisted her journey was unquestionably a physical one. What Allison produced as "evidence" was circumstantial. The love beads could have been hers; the picture could have been bought or borrowed and, certainly, she could have written the prose on the back of it. But it was the lapel watch that disturbed the doctor. No amount of cleaning could have made a watch that old appear brand new. Yes, Allison could have had it made, but such an act would be a premeditated one, the act of a sick mind. Reva Mitchell did not believe Allison was sick and therein was the controversy.

"If I could see the photograph taken in the café," Dr. Mitchell said as they neared their final visits together, "it might clear up some inconsistencies in my mind."

"How?" The idea of stealing the picture from Frances's album did not appeal to Allison.

"It would add to the foundation of your existence in 1944. I would be more inclined to—"

"Believe me?"

"Maybe."

"You are asking me to steal, Dr. Mitchell."

"And you are asking me to believe you traveled back forty-eight years, Allison. Under the circumstances, I consider it a fair exchange."

After the session, the limousine pulled up in front of the brownstone. Mrs. G. was coming down the front steps and hailed Allison.

"Traveling in style these days, Allison, aren't we?"

"ChemProbe is picking up the tab while I'm doing research."

"I hardly see you much these days." Mrs. G. fumbled around in her large bag and pulled out a pair of gloves. "I'm on my way to the market and then to see a friend in the hospital."

"Nothing serious, I hope," Allison said, her mind racing as to how to get into Frances's apartment while she was away.

"Lois is overweight and smokes too much, but she'll be fine." She tightened the top button of her coat. "I'm glad I caught you."

"Why is that?"

"I'm expecting a Sears delivery—a new chair for the living room. They promised to come before five... I can't wait much longer. Do you mind?"

"Mind what?" Allison asked, still not making the connection.

"Letting them in, of course. I left the key in an envelope in your mailbox."

"Thank God," Allison mumbled.

"What was that, dear?"

"I said, how odd. Sears is usually reliable." She started up the steps. "Don't worry; I'll let them in."

Allison waited until Mrs. G. was gone before opening her mailbox. Once in the apartment, she steered immediately to the bookcase for the photo album and flipped through to the café picture. She was slipping it off the page when the Sears people arrived. Both tasks accomplished, she took to bed early, folding the envelope with the key back into Mrs. G.'s box on her way up. Sleep was difficult as her excitement increased. Dr. Mitchell would be hard pressed to refute the existence of the picture.

CHAPTER FOURTEEN

"Now what do you think?" Allison asked Reva Mitchell the next day.

"I don't know what to say," the doctor answered honestly. "The resemblance is uncanny. Can I keep this a few days?"

"As long as you return it before December twenty-fourth." Allison was fully aware of Reva Mitchell's intentions. The woman was going to have the photo analyzed.

On December twenty-third, Dr. Reva Mitchell reported her evaluation of Allison McKay to Horace Banks. Clearly Allison was in control of all her faculties. In Dr. Mitchell's estimation, Allison was intelligent and not easy prey to fantasy. Further, the doctor did not deem the concept of going back in time an unlikely scenario. Many people had done it through hypnosis, she insisted, and Allison's clear recollection of experience in 1944 could be factual, especially in light of the "evidence" that had been presented.

The capsule had not physically or mentally impaired Allison, and Reva Mitchell strongly felt Horace Banks was onto something notable—most definitely worth pursuing if Allison McKay was a willing subject. Her recommendation was to permit Allison to take the journey with a full supply of forty-eight-hour capsules.

After intense dispute with Robin Page, Horace Banks telephoned Allison on December twenty-fourth and advised her of his colleague's findings.

"I have generated enough capsules to last past age one hundred, God willing," Horace relayed over the telephone. "Though Dr. Page thinks it highly improper, we will permit the experiment if you will agree to sign a few documents."

"To protect ChemProbe?"

"You, my dear, to protect you, as well. That's the only stipulation: that you sign the paperwork before your...trip."

Allison heaved a heavy sigh. "Thank God. I will gladly sign my life away."

"You may be doing just that." Horace cleared his throat. "You indicated you had a place in mind for the experiment."

"Yes. Meet me in front of the brownstone at seven o'clock." She hesitated a moment. "I know it's Christmas Eve, Dr. Banks, and I'm sorry to take you away from your family."

"No need to apologize, Allison. We will be at the building at the appointed time."

If ever there really was a cloud nine, Allison McKay was on it. She had prepared herself for this last journey by hunting through more New York shops for 1940's clothing and accessories, and even had the foresight to purchase appropriate Christmas gifts to deliver when she returned to 1944.

Her hair in a neat pageboy, Allison checked herself one more time in the foyer mirror. She was wearing a red dress not unlike the one she had borrowed from Frances that first day, comfortable matching pumps, the lapel watch, and a heavy red cloak, its hood framed with white fur. She smiled impishly at her reflection. *I could give Little Red Riding Hood a run for her money in this get up!* Locking the door behind her, she tossed the key into her mailbox and knocked on Mrs. G.'s door.

"Allison, my goodness, if I didn't know better, I'd think you were her!" she whispered through a crack in the door.

"May I come in?"

"No!" Mrs. G. continued in a whisper. "He's here! And he mustn't see you, especially with you looking the way you do."

He's right inside! My God, he's within reach!

"I came to say good-bye."

"Where are you off to? A costume party?"

"You might say that." Allison tried to peak in, but Mrs. G. stood firmly blocking her view. "I just wanted to wish you a Merry Christmas."

"Merry Christmas, Allison." Frances Giovani quickly closed the door.

Light of heart and filled with expectation, Allison swiftly walked out of the building and down the steps to the pile of boxes and garbage awaiting pick up in front of the brownstone.

Frances Giovani pulled back a portion of her living room curtain and curiously watched Allison greet the two doctors.

"You sure you want to go through with this?" Robin Page asked while pulling on a pair of warm gloves.

"I'm ready when you are, Dr. Banks," Allison said, ignoring Robin's question.

Horace Banks handed her a neatly wrapped package containing the supply of capsules, and she tucked it carefully into her cloth shopping bag. The wind whipped around the three as they stood in the gutter in front of the brownstone, the inquisitive Mrs. G. still unseen at her window. A piece of newspaper flew past, slapping against Allison's feet, and Robin Page kicked it away as he stepped closer and handed her a Thermos.

"If you insist on doing this, might as well go remembering my delicious hot chocolate," he said with a smile.

"I know this is difficult for you, Robin, and I don't really hate you, I—"

"Forget it. The longer we stand here, the better the chance of freezing to death."

Horace Banks handed her a capsule. "God be with you."

Allison sat down on a box with the Thermos and swallowed the pill. Forty-five minutes later, Robin Page looked at his watch. Small, thick flakes of snow began to fall over them, and Allison tightened a hand around her hood.

"Come on, Allison, this is not—"

"Maybe it's because I'm not sick anymore." She turned pleading eyes on them, the white flakes lacing her long eyelashes.

"Somehow I doubt that," Robin replied.

Allison cast him a look, and Horace shook his head.

"Sorry, I didn't mean anything. I promised to be professional about this," Robin apologized.

"If you sit out here long enough, you'll catch pneumonia," Horace offered gently, his snow-laden hat heavily descending down over his ears.

Robin rolled a garbage can over to the gutter and began tossing in whatever he could find to make a fire. "Might as well do the sensible thing; we've got to keep warm some way. We've been here almost an hour now, and the snow is falling heavier."

"No!" Allison said with alarm. "I mean, not here, not so close to me."

Both doctors rolled the can through the blanket of snow and closer to the sidewalk. Together they fed the fire, rubbing their hands briskly in front of it, their bodies nearly pressed against it.

"Ahh…CHOO!"

They turned, eyes squinting through the yellow flames, the snow a flurry of white in front of them. Allison McKay was gone, leaving only snow-covered boxes in her wake.

CHAPTER FIFTEEN

SWOOSH!

The blocks under John Minetti's car were engulfed in flames, and a uniformed air raid warden was dousing out the fire, calling to the small crowd that had mingled around it.

"It's okay. Everything's under control."

Allison had misjudged the distance of Johnny's car and instead of finding herself in it, she was sitting just beyond it. She got up and dusted the snow from her cloak. She was afraid something like this would happen. Fortunately, the warden had done a good job, and now Johnny's precious car sat to the ground, the only destruction the burnt blocks it was once propped up on.

Frances was at the window attempting to see what all the fuss was about, but the neighbors mingling out front were in her way. She shrugged it off and drew down the blackout shade.

"You okay?" the man was asking.

"Yes, thank you," Allison replied.

"Are you sure you're okay, Mrs. Carmella?" he repeated.

Mrs. Carmella? Allison watched as the warden helped an elderly woman to her feet. *Doesn't he see me? I'm right here!* She tapped him on the shoulder. "Excuse me."

Her finger passed right through him.

Oh, my God, I'm not here yet! Allison fearfully looked down at her hands as they faded in and out right before here eyes. Something was very, very wrong.

"Can't imagine what would cause such a thing," the Warden continued once he had Mrs. Carmella on her feet.

Allison picked up her parcels and groaned.

Now I know why that psychic told me to travel light! She looked around at the dwindling crowd. If they couldn't see her, how would Johnny and Frances be able to? The capsule wasn't fully working, and she hadn't the faintest idea why!

"Shouldn't you be inside somewhere?" he asked with concern. "There's a war on, you know," he said, plodding through the snow.

"Yes, of course," Mrs. Carmella answered as she turned and walked slowly up the steps of the brownstone next door.

Allison stepped carefully through the deep snow, her new pumps soaked through to her feet, and cursed herself for not thinking to wear boots—not that it mattered if she wasn't really here. She groaned inwardly and walked up the front steps of the Minetti brownstone. Opening the door, she trudged up to the third floor apartment with her cumbersome packages. At the top, she stopped in front of the door to catch her breath and placed the shopping bag down on the welcome mat. After a moment she wiped her feet on the mat and rang the bell. John Minetti opened the door, a cane lending him support.

"Merry Christmas."

John looked straight through her. "Merry Christmas, Lois."

Lois? Allison turned around. Directly behind her stood Lois, several presents in her hands. As Johnny took the packages from her, Allison slipped inside with them.

"You weren't expecting me, were you, Johnny?" Lois asked, slightly miffed. "You usually use the back door, Lois."

"That's not what I mean, and you know it." Lois placed her gifts under the tree in the living room.

"I was expecting Ali," he said, sitting down in the easy chair and picking up his drink from the end table beside it.

Frances came into the room wearing a colorful red smock. "Merry Christmas, Lois." She pecked Lois on the cheek. "Why the front door, unusual for you, isn't it?"

"I gather that neither of you were expecting me." Lois followed Frances into the kitchen. Allison followed them both.

"John is beside himself. I hate to see him so sad, especially during the holidays," Frances said, bending to check the lasagna in the oven. "Every time the door bell rings, he runs to answer, and every time, he's disappointed."

Allison watched as Lois helped herself to an open bottle of red wine and poured herself a glass. She sat down at the kitchen table and lit a cigarette.

"What's it been…a month? She hasn't called or even written. You'd think she'd have the courtesy to thank you for helping her out."

Bitch! Allison pushed the ashtray, and it fell to the floor. Lois picked it up.

"Don't be so hard on Ali."

"I'm only speaking the truth."

"We don't know what the truth is, Lois. Besides, I've a feeling she may still show up."

Thanks, Frances. I knew I could count on you. Allison paced up and down the length of the kitchen. Should she take another pill? No, she might go back further, and she liked it fine in 1944—but not this way, never this way.

Tiring of the kitchen conversation, Allison walked into the living room. Johnny was putting a record on the phonograph.

The band swelled and "Sentimental Journey" floated up to her ears, and a sweeter sound she had never heard. Johnny began to softly hum the song, and Allison felt her heart sink. She recovered quickly when Lois came into the room.

"You still owe me a dance, Sailor," she said, her big bosom fleshing out of her too-tight dress.

He's not going to dance with her to our song! He just can't!

Allison stepped between them like thin air. Then she thought of the ashtray and how she was able to touch it. Obviously, while in this state of transparency she was able to touch objects, just not people. As Johnny's hand hesitantly started to go around Lois's waist, Allison picked up an ashtray and hauled it in their direction.

"What the hell—" The ashtray hit Lois squarely in the legs, cutting into a calf. She bent down and rubbed it.

"You're bleeding," Johnny said with little emotion.

Frances came running from the kitchen. "What happened?"

Lois was licking her fingers and rubbing her calf.

"Your guess is as good as mine." Johnny shrugged.

"That ashtray came flying out of nowhere is what happened!"

"Calm down, Lois." Frances hustled off to the kitchen and returned with some ice. "Ashtrays don't fly."

"Well, that one did." She pointed to the one on the floor, her eyes angry slits. "If the two of you don't want me here, just say so!"

Allison sat down beside the tree and smiled broadly. *That's one for Ali!* Her smile quickly faded when Johnny knelt down to rub Lois's leg. *Ooh! All I managed to do was get her sympathy.* She got up and stood beside Johnny who was lighting Lois's cigarette. Allison blew a full gale into the direction of the match. The flame went out. Johnny struck another match, and another, but it never managed to reach Lois's cigarette before disappearing.

It was several moments before any of them realized the telephone was ringing. Frances hastily picked it up.

"Just a minute." She handed the phone to Johnny.

"It's for you. Our wonderful warden needs to have a word with you," she said, handing him the telephone.

"Yes?" Johnny nodded his head a few times. "I understand. What do you think caused it?" He switched the telephone to his other ear. "No, I couldn't answer that either. I'll look into it in the morning. Yes…Merry Christmas."

"What was that all about?" Frances asked, seated beside the injured Lois, both of them puffing stacks of cigarette smoke into the air. Allison waved it away. A good sign, she could smell.

I was able to smell in 1969, too, but I still wasn't seen or heard.

"The warden says the blocks under the Chevy caught fire."

Frances looked up. "So, that's what all the commotion was earlier." She stamped out her cigarette. "A few were mingling out front just before Lois came." They both looked at Lois.

"Why look at me? I had nothing to do with it."

"I told him I'd check into it in the morning," Johnny answered. "Is dinner ready yet?" Aided by his cane, he limped into the dining room and sat down at the head of the table.

Lois hobbled herself over and sat in close proximity to him. Johnny filled four glasses from a fresh bottle of wine. Lois looked curiously at the fourth glass.

"Are we expecting someone?"

"You never know," he answered.

"Well, I know Jerry isn't due home, so who is the mystery guest?" She brought the wine to her lips and swallowed it in two gulps.

Allison sat down, careful to not let Johnny see the chair move away from the table. But Lois saw it—so clearly that her face went stark white, her hands flying to her mouth.

"Lois, are you sure you're all right?" Johnny asked.

She rubbed her eyes. "I thought I saw that chair move."

Frances set the casserole in the center of the table and pulled off her apron. "How much have you had to drink tonight?"

"I'm telling you that chair moved away from the table and then back in again! And for your information, I've had two martinis and two glasses of wine."

"That could do it." For the first time since Allison returned, Johnny was laughing.

Allison watched as Frances cut squares of lasagna in the casserole and then served each plate. It smelled so good she wished she could reach out and taste some for herself. She leaned her elbow on the table and rested her chin on her hand. In a way it was intriguing to listen in on conversation when no one knew you were there.

Despite his "loss" over her, Johnny appeared to have a healthy appetite, as did Frances. But Lois just moved her fork around the plate, bringing very little to her mouth.

"I don't understand all this, Johnny," she said. "I mean, here you are mooning over someone you knew a couple of days, on leave no less!"

"I'm not mooning, Lois; I'm eating."

"Ali is a lovely girl," Frances interjected. "We didn't know her long, but I consider her a friend."

"Then where is your friend now, Frances?" Lois asked impatiently. "Your so-called friend used you both."

"Why?" It was Johnny who posed the question. "I don't know."

"Then shut up, Lois," he said harshly.

"John!" Frances reprimanded. "That's no way to speak to Lois."

"It's the only way I can think of," he countered. Then he turned to Lois. "You know, you can be a real pain in the ass when you want to. Weren't you ever in love? Don't you have feelings for anybody but yourself?"

Lois got up from the table, and Allison noticed tears in her eyes. "I've been in love, Johnny, and whether you believe it or not, I do have feelings." She came around the table and kissed Frances on the cheek. "The lasagna was good, Franny, but I've suddenly lost my appetite."

For the first time since she met Lois, Allison actually felt sorry for her. It was obvious the woman was in love with Johnny, and he had been cruel—something Allison thought he could never be.

It proves I don't really know him. Maybe I don't even want to. It's my fault. I've done this to him — hardened him.

Frances moved away from the table to walk Lois to the door. When she returned, she sat down silently, but Allison was sure sparks would soon fly.

"John Minetti, I'm ashamed of you. You were very mean to Lois."

Johnny filled his glass again and drank the wine, quickly refilling. "No one invited her."

"She needs no invitation!" Frances slammed her fist down on the table. "This is my house. Papa left it to me, and I will not have you treat my friends like dirt! Especially considering that Lois's rent helps us to keep this place. Otherwise you would not have a home to come back to!"

"Now don't get excited, Sis. Think of the baby," he said gently.

Frances got up and removed the plates at once. "Look, Johnny, I miss Ali, too, but there is nothing I can do to bring her back. If she wanted to return, she would. And maybe, just maybe, she couldn't… because she has a family and that family might easily include a husband and children. Think of that while you wallow in self pity!" She cleared the table swiftly with several trips to the kitchen. Johnny tried to assist, but Frances was having none of it. "If you want dessert, you'll have to help yourself. I'm going to bed."

Alone in the living room, Johnny switched on the floor lamp and sat in his chair. Allison looked on as he reached into his shirt pocket for his cigarettes and lit one. Then he pulled out a piece of paper.

My note!

I remember home.

He read the three words again, "I remember home," and then crumpled it into a little ball before tossing it into the ashtray.

Who knew I was writing a genuine "Dear John" letter at the time?

Allison shook her head. There was no use hanging around inside the apartment. She was confused and hurt. Dejected, she walked through the front door and down the steps. Horace Banks and Robin Page had been right, and she was too selfish to listen. They had warned her, and those warnings went unheeded. Now she was alone, in a limbo of sorts, not able to live fully in any time, not even her own. And she had left a drastic mark on the lives of three people—people who were warm and loving—who had taken her into their lives without question. They didn't deserve this—not even Lois.

She sat on the steps, watching the snow fall for a long time, her eyes fixed on Johnny's car, which had now settled into the snow, the blocks under it mere strips of wood. She didn't know where to go or what to do. She got up and walked over to the car. She opened the unlocked door, and she slipped into the front seat with her parcels.

How long will I have to wait? she thought while locking herself inside the car. The bigger question was: how long before something will happen? Maybe nothing is going to happen. *Maybe I'm destined to be the captive of time. Maybe I'll never* be *again!* The thoughts terrified her. Her worries before had been not having enough time. Time was still the enemy, but now there was too much of it.

Oh, God, please help me. I promise to be a kinder, gentler Allison.

The longer she dwelled on her circumstances, the harder she cried, until she cried herself to sleep.

CHAPTER SIXTEEN

The next morning Johnny went down to check out the Chevy. He fumbled with the frozen lock, cursing loudly until the lock gave way. He swung the door open.

"Ali!"

For Allison it was more a scream than her name, and she shot up from the front seat, hitting her head on the dashboard in the process.

Johnny drew her into his arms and kissed her long and hard. "Ali…oh, Ali, I thought I'd lost you," he murmured while rocking her back and forth.

Thank you, God. He can see me…touch me. She cried softly, her eyes swollen and puffy.

"What the hell are you doing out here?"

"I came to see you last night. Your car was on fire, and after everyone left I opened the door to check the inside." That sounded plausible. "I don't remember anything after that. I guess maybe I fell asleep?"

"Oh, my poor baby!" He kissed her again before sweeping her into his arms and up the steps of the brownstone.

"My packages!"

"We'll get them later." He kissed her again, and soon they were at the apartment door. "Sis, it's Ali, she's come back!" he called, pain shooting up his leg as he set her down and quickly reached for his cane.

"Johnny, you're hurt."

"Honey, I'm fine. The cane is only temporary." He kissed her again, gently removing her hooded cloak. "We didn't hear from you; Franny was worried about you, and so was I. We thought—"

"Shh." Allison put a wet gloved finger to his lips and kissed him. "None of that matters now. I'm here, and I have no intention of leaving you ever again."

CHAPTER SEVENTEEN

"Sis, this crazy war has taken enough time from me. I love Ali and, well, we've decided to get married," Johnny blurted out over dinner two days later. "And we want you to be there with us when we do, don't we, Ali?"

Allison's eyes watched the hands of the clock in the dining room with anticipation. Soon she would have to take the first pill from Dr. Banks's package. Should she do so in front of Johnny and Frances? Wouldn't they question her need for medication? As the long hand met the twelve, the tiny grandfather clock chimed seven times.

"Ali?" Johnny smiled nervously. "You haven't changed your mind, have you, darling?"

"What? No, of course I haven't changed my mind. Excuse me a moment." Allison pushed her chair back and got up from the table, heading quickly for the bedroom and the time capsules.

Frances and Johnny looked at each other questioningly. Frances touched a hand to his shoulder as he started to get up and gently pushed him down.

"I'll see to her. I'll bet she caught cold sleeping the night in the Chevy."

In the bedroom, Allison carefully opened Dr. Banks's parcel. Each capsule was inside its own slim test tube, and each test tube had been individually wrapped in heavy-duty packing material. Allison smiled. Horace was expecting this to be a bumpy journey. With the shake of her head, she unrolled a tube. Pulling out the stopper, she spilled the capsule into the palm of her hand. *Water. I'm going to need water to wash this down…*

"Ali, are you all right?" Frances appeared in the doorway, a glass of water in her hands.

"I am now." Allison gratefully accepted the water as Frances sat beside her on the bed. With a quick pop into her mouth, she swallowed the capsule and finished the remainder of the water. "Thanks, Frances."

"What's wrong, Ali? What was that pill for?" Frances asked with concern. "If you're not well, we can call for the doctor."

"I'm fine." Allison touched a hand to Frances. "It was a vitamin."

"A vitamin?"

"Yes…iron…you see, I'm anemic. Just a tad, but enough to have to take a supplement." Allison's mind raced in circles. Did they have supplements in the forties? They weren't the most health conscious of generations. "I take one pill every two days so I don't get too tired," she added quickly.

Frances got up. "Well, if that's all it was, why did you rush from the dining room the way you did? You scared us half to death," she reprimanded.

"I'm sorry." Allison tucked Horace's package back into her shopping bag.

"If you need to take the pill, you should have it with you at the table." Frances headed for the door.

"I will." Allison followed Frances back to the dining room.

Johnny pulled Allison's chair out and eased her to the table with a kiss on the cheek. "Everything okay, Sweetheart?" he asked with concern.

"Yes." Allison looked to Frances who went on to explain Allison's iron deficiency.

"I read a study in *Reader's Digest* about this very thing, but I didn't know they had a pill for it already."

"Science is an interesting subject," Allison said, spooning mashed potatoes into her mouth.

Johnny put down his fork and smiled. "There is so much I have to learn about you, Ali." He picked up his glass of wine and took a sip. "Liking science, for instance. I never thought of women as being interested in science, at least not judging from the women I've gone with."

"John, I'm surprised at you!" Frances laughed. "Women are responsible for making the very planes being flown during wartime; that shows more of an interest in science than in baking cookies."

"And that's only because men aren't around to do it," Johnny answered.

"What a sexist thing to say!" Allison admonished.

"A what?" Johnny looked at her strangely. "A what thing to say?"

Allison bit her tongue. Women's liberation was a long way off back in 1944; she'd have to be more careful. "It's a word I made up. It means you have a certain image of women that puts them beneath you as a man."

"There's nothing wrong with that!" Johnny winked, and Frances laughed.

"That's exactly what I'm talking about! You just made a joke at the expense of women."

Frances began clearing away the dishes. "Oh, Ali, you're funny! Johnny was just being funny is all. Don't be so serious."

Johnny helped Allison with the remainder from the dining room and joined them in the kitchen. "Speaking of being serious, I suppose I should apologize to Lois."

"I suppose you should," Frances answered. "You were very unkind to her Christmas Eve."

Johnny bent down to kiss Allison, who was at the sink rinsing dishes. "I won't be long."

"What's that's all about?" Allison asked, feigning innocence as she watched Johnny leave by the back door.

"Johnny was very rude to Lois. He hurt her." Frances picked up a dish for drying. "I won't stand for my friends being hurt."

Allison nodded. "Neither would I." She handed a wet plate to Frances. "She's in love with him, you know."

"I know…but he's in love with you." Frances stacked the plate onto her already dried pile. "I know my brother, Ali, and nothing will ever change that. It was love at first sight for Johnny, and I suspect for you, too."

Allison nodded. "I hope you're right. I hope he is madly in love with me, Frances."

CHAPTER EIGHTEEN

Lois forgave Johnny, if only to find out more about Ali. In the guise of friendship, she offered to throw a small party for the couple. Allison relented only after much persistence by Frances.

"It's nice of Lois to make such an offer, and nice of you to invite her to be a witness at the ceremony. This neighborhood could use a morale boost," Frances said.

How long Allison would be able to keep Lois at bay she didn't know, but she was going to do her best to dodge her questions. She didn't share Frances' liking for the silver-tongued Lois and found the relationship between the women difficult to understand.

Allison had managed to remain solidly in 1944 for almost a full week, and Johnny wanted to be married in City Hall that Sunday, New Year's Eve.

He had spent the afternoon of the party with some Navy buddies to say good-bye to bachelorhood. When he came home, he was too drunk to attend Lois's party. For the first time in the short while they'd known each other, Allison was furious. Her fury was not so much that Johnny was drunk but that he wouldn't be escorting them to the party. It was his party, too, she argued.

"Just let me get a few winks, honey. I'll come down to Lois's place later."

Though the blackout shades in Lois's apartment were pulled down, the party inside was far from dark. Available men were scarce, but Lois managed quite nicely, and much to Ali's surprise, there were more men in attendance than women.

"Come on in," Lois said, answering the door in a tight black evening dress cut low enough to expose a bit more of her ample bosom; a slit on each side cut its way up each thigh. "Where's your better—I mean, other—half?"

"Sleeping off a drunk." It was Frances who answered as she pushed Allison gently into the room.

"He's going to show up, isn't he?" Lois put an arm around Allison's shoulder.

"He'll be down later."

"Good. It just wouldn't be the same without him." Lois led them over to a punch bowl. "Everyone chipped in for the booze. Mrs. Carmella made the finger sandwiches. Help yourself."

"It was generous of you to go through all this trouble," Allison said in a vain attempt at small talk.

Lois reached over, picked up a sandwich, and popped it into her mouth. "Oh, honey, I've got lots of time and lots of energy for putting together a bash!" She smiled sweetly. "Besides, Franny tells me you get so tired you're popping pills to keep you going. Sure hope you're feeling okay."

Words failed Allison. She knew her mistake immediately. The two women were close enough for Frances to share her concern over the "iron" pills.

"Be right back...got some chip and dip in the kitchen."

"Can I help?" Frances offered.

"No, no. I've got it covered. Enjoy the party."

They watched her wiggle through the crowd, hesitating a moment between two sailors and fawning over a soldier before slipping into the kitchen.

CHAPTER NINETEEN

Upstairs, Johnny slept soundly in his own bed for the first time since Allison's return. The studio couch was okay, but he missed sleeping in a real bed — his bed. In a few days, he would be sharing a bed with Ali. Raising his hands up over his head, he smiled broadly. It was going to be heaven sharing a bed with his new wife. With her beautiful face etched behind his eyelids, John Minetti closed his eyes and drifted off with a long sigh.

Determined to have a few last moments alone with Johnny, Lois slipped out the back door and up to the Giovani apartment. She found him asleep in the bedroom and bent over him, a hand gingerly pushing away a lock of his hair. Slowly, she reached a palm to his cheek and kissed him. He responded with half-closed eyes and touched a hand to her face.

"Ali, oh, baby…"

With injured pride, Lois pulled away from him. "It's not Ali, Johnny," she said indignantly. "Ali isn't the only one who knows how to kiss a man."

"Lois?" Johnny struggled to open his eyes.

Lois took his face into her hands and kissed his mouth hard. "That's right, baby; it's Lois. And Lois knows just how Johnny likes it," she whispered.

"I'm not that drunk!" With both hands, Johnny roughly forced her away.

Lois sat up, her pinned curls coming away from the sparkle of netting that held them in place. "You bastard." Her hand flew to his face, and he caught it before its sting could meet his cheek.

"Leave me alone, Lois." He turned on his side. "What did you come up here for anyway? Besides the obvious."

"For Ali's iron pills," she said, thinking quickly. Without turning, Johnny waved a hand. "Try there," he said sleepily.

Lois knelt down beside the bed and opened Allison's shopping bag. "What have we here?" Digging deep, she pulled out the package of capsules. "So many pills! They must do more than what she claims. Why else would she have so many of them and so safely tucked away?"

"What?" Johnny mumbled.

"Nothing. Go to sleep."

He turned onto his stomach with a long, grateful sigh.

Next to the capsules was Allison's journal. "What have we here? Little Ali's diary maybe?" Lois took it in her hands, opened to the first page, and began to read.

CHAPTER TWENTY

The party appeared to be winding down in the apartment below. Both Frances and Ali were concerned over Lois's disappearance.

"She was going for chip and dip, wasn't she?" Frances asked.

"Maybe." Allison put her cup down on the coffee table. "You see any chip and dip?"

"Nope."

"I'll be right back, Frances." Smiling at the well-wishers, she slipped into the kitchen. Frances followed closely behind.

"Well, where is she?" Frances asked, her hands gently rubbing her growing belly, a habit she had taken to in times of stress.

"I think I know." Allison turned to her friend. "You stay here and play the gracious hostess for us. I'm going to get Johnny. I've a feeling I'll find Lois with him."

"Oh, Ali, don't be ridiculous! Johnny wouldn't—"

"I didn't say Johnny would be doing anything, Frances, but I don't trust Lois. Now stay here and keep these people happy for me. I promise to be right down with Johnny, even if I have to drag him out of that bed. I just hope he's alone."

"Oh, Ali!" Frances's hand flew to her mouth. She quickly took to a kitchen chair, sitting down with a thump.

"Be careful! You have someone else to think about," Allison warned. "Everything will be all right."

"Let me come with you," Frances pleaded.

"No," Allison said sternly. "I don't think it would be wise in your condition. Stress isn't good for the baby."

"In my condition? I'm having a baby, not a heart attack!" Frances rose angrily from the kitchen chair. "That apartment up there is mine, and if something is wrong, I want to know about it!"

"All right, come along then."

Without saying a word to the remaining guests, they left through the back door and climbed the stairs to the Giovani apartment. The door was open, and Johnny was in the shower, singing. Allison marched into the bathroom and pulled back the shower curtain to the shock of a blushing Johnny.

"Okay, where is she?"

Soap was stinging his eyes, and he didn't know what to do first, cover his nakedness or rinse the soap.

"What the hell—"

Realizing that women didn't do such things in 1944, Allison was now blushing too. With a quick down jerk of her head, she tried to explain. "Where's Lois?"

He turned the water off. "I don't know. Mind handing me a towel?"

"Towel…right…here." Head still down, she tossed him a towel.

"You're full of surprises, Ali," he said stepping out of the shower, the towel wrapped casually around him. "You can look up now."

Frances knocked on the open bathroom door. "Ali? Johnny?"

"Be right out, Sis."

Mortified, Allison meekly followed him into the bedroom where he sat down on the bed, his hands rustling through his thick, curly hair. Frances stood by the door and shook her head.

"We were sure Lois was up here with you."

"She was." He lit a cigarette and exhaled a circle of smoke.

"Where is she now?" Allison asked.

"Your guess is as good as mine."

Frances looked at Allison. "Well, if you're not going to ask, I will." She turned to Johnny. "What was she doing up here?"

"How the hell should I know?" He stamped the cigarette out into the ashtray where it smoldered angrily. "I resent being questioned like this!"

Allison rushed over to him by the bed. "I'm sorry, Johnny, but I don't trust Lois."

"Who does?" He smoothed his hand over hers. "I told you I love you, and I asked you to marry me.

What more can I say or do to prove to you I have no interest in any other woman, especially Lois?"

"Nothing. I mean, I just wish I knew what Lois—" Allison's eyes caught sight of her shopping bag, which was now turned over on its side, and was gripped with fear.

"Look, she was here, and she apparently left." Johnny got up and moved over to the closet for a pair of pants. While they looked away, he slipped them on. "She said she came up for one of your iron pills."

Frances sighed. "Is that all? Well, she must be in the building somewhere."

Allison rushed over to her shopping bag. One of the vials was gone as was her journal. The question was no longer *where* Lois was, but *when*.

CHAPTER TWENTY-ONE

"Forty-eight hours, Mrs. G. That's how long before we can deal with your friend as a missing person." Frances had Johnny call Captain Ramsey, one of New York's finest. "I know Lois; we all know Lois. This wouldn't be the first time she disappeared," he said while drinking a cup of coffee in the Giovani kitchen.

"Captain, we haven't heard from Lois since the party on Thursday."

"So? It's only Friday."

"My brother is getting married New Year's Eve, and Lois was a last minute witness for the ceremony. She has to be at City Hall on Sunday and we haven't heard from her."

"You're a lucky man, Johnny Minetti. My hats off to you."

"Thanks, Ramsey." John shook his hand. "I called you in because I didn't want to upset Frances. My sister's condition…well, you know."

Ramsey nodded conspiratorially.

"What's this big fuss over my condition, damn it?"

"Mothers-to-be are a bit sensitive, Mrs. G."

"I am not being sensitive; I'm being concerned," Frances answered in frustration. "And how the hell would you know, Ramsey? You give birth lately? Hiding something from us, are you?"

Allison sat down beside Frances at the kitchen table. "Lois will be back, Frances. You have to have faith."

"Sounds like sound advice, Sis." Johnny remarked.

"You say that with such confidence. You don't know that." She ignored him and faced Allison.

"She will be back, and it will be before the wedding."

Captain Ramsey accepted a refill of coffee. "And how do you know that Miss…"

"Allison McKay." She extended her hand. "I think Lois feels rejected," she said quickly. "She needed time to get over her crush on Johnny. She'll be back."

What disturbed Allison most was where Lois moved through time. Was the capsule capable of only moving back, as she had assumed? Or could it move a person forward, through his or her own time? If that was the case, Lois could be in 1992. A little knowledge was a dangerous thing, and with Lois it could be catastrophic.

Damn it, Lois, where are you?

CHAPTER TWENTY-TWO

At nine o'clock Saturday evening, Lois rematerialized back in Ali's room in the Giovani apartment. She stood near the dresser, still wearing her provocative black dress, her face pale, eyes wide, a smile on her ruby-red lips. Her tight pin curls were now loose and unruly, and she had scratches all over her once neatly painted leg make up.

That get-up must have been some jolt to the eyes, Allison thought angrily.

"I've been waiting for you," Allison said from her position on the bed, pillows propped up comfortably behind her. "Where have you been, Lois?"

"Wouldn't you like to know?" She turned and faced the mirror, raising her hands high above her head before finger combing her blond locks. "I'll tell you something, Ali," she turned from her reflection. "Excuse me, Allison…I like where I've been."

"Oh God." Allison groaned. Her fear had been realized.

"And where was that?"

Lois laughed heartily. "You're a pip, you know that?"

Allison leaped from the bed, her movements quick and angry. "Don't play games with me, Lois. This is serious business." With both hands she pushed Lois hard against the dresser. "Now, stop being a smart ass and talk to me!"

"Hey—watch the merchandise!" Lois straightened the hem of her dress and walked over to the bed. "You've got a helluva nerve, considering." She sat down and reached for Johnny's cigarettes on the night table and fired one up. "I mean, after all, you don't belong here, do you?" Inhaling deeply, she exhaled a cloud of smoke into Allison's face.

"You're trying my patience, Lois. You really are." Allison remained standing, her hands on her hips. "I wouldn't be so smug if I were you."

"Oh? Why's that?"

"Because tomorrow Johnny and I will be married."

"Not if I can help it."

"There's nothing you can do about it Lois."

"I can tell him the truth."

"And you think he'd believe you?"

Lois hadn't thought of that. With a long sigh, she leaned against the pillows of the bed.

"Well?" Allison continued.

"No," Lois answered simply.

Allison sat on the bed and faced her squarely. "You are taking this all very lightly. You have no idea what that pill you took is capable of doing to you," Allison said in all seriousness.

Lois leaned forward and grasped Allison's hands. "I'm okay, kiddo. I went ahead in time. I had a chance to see the future! I don't know how, but I do know I'd like to go there again." She took another drag from the cigarette before putting it out. "What I don't understand is why you went back and I went forward. You only wrote about going back in time, not ahead."

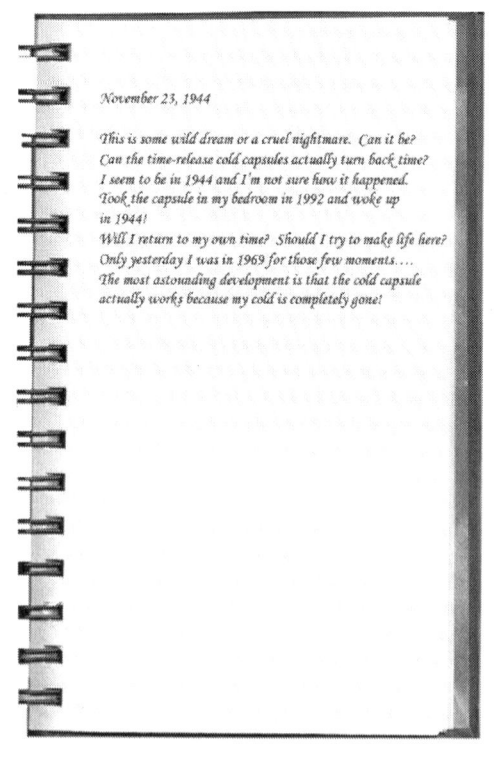

> *November 23, 1944*
>
> *This is some wild dream or a cruel nightmare. Can it be? Can the time-release cold capsules actually turn back time? I seem to be in 1944 and I'm not sure how it happened. Took the capsule in my bedroom in 1992 and woke up in 1944!*
> *Will I return to my own time? Should I try to make life here? Only yesterday I was in 1969 for those few moments....*
> *The most astounding development is that the cold capsule actually works because my cold is completely gone!*

"The journal," Allison whispered half to herself. "Yes, well, I guess I was wrong." Allison's wheels were spinning. How could she put the fear of God into Lois? She tried another approach. "In the future you're in the hospital, Lois, did you know that?"

"What do you mean?"

"You're still alive. You're overweight and old, Lois, suffering in a hospital. There can't be two of you running around the city of New York."

"Then I'll just have to kill my old self, won't I?" Lois giggled.

"Shh," Allison scolded. "You'll wake Johnny and Frances." Explaining the idea of time travel was not going to be easy. "If you kill your 'old' self, as you call it, your young self may not survive."

"You don't know that. In fact, you don't know much of anything, do you?"

With a fling of her wrist, Allison slapped Lois across the face and forced her against the pillows. "I know one thing. You are tampering with something you do not understand, and I won't have it, do you hear me! I won't have it!" She slapped her again, but Lois was quick in defense and with a one long leg, she kicked Allison squarely in the stomach, overpowering her.

"You bitch! Who do you think you're kidding? You just want Johnny all to yourself." She was on her feet now, standing over the injured Allison who held her hands to her stomach in an attempt to catch her breath.

"This is not about Johnny!" Allison managed.

"What a joke you are, Allison McKay!" With another kick to Allison, Lois hurried over to the shopping bag and took the package of vials from it.

"No! Please!" Allison pleaded, still suffering on the floor of the bedroom. "You don't know what you're doing! I need them!" She struggled to get up, faltered, and fell back down.

"Tough!" Lois clutched the package to her chest and rushed out of the room.

Tears streaming down her cheeks, Allison strove to get up, one hand gripping a leg of the bed. Slowly, she raised her injured body up and, feeling a trickle of wetness from her mouth, touched a hand to her lips. *Blood. Oh, God, what am I to do?*

The capsules were gone, and in less than an hour, she would be too.

CHAPTER TWENTY-THREE

Allison awoke the morning of her wedding in her own bed and in her own time in pain and remorse. She raised herself up with difficulty, pain shooting through her stomach, and dully moved from the bedroom to the living room. She picked up the telephone and dialed ChemProbe.

"Robin Page speaking."

"Robin?" she questioned weakly.

"Allison?"

"Robin…please come to the brownstone…please come right now."

As darkness embraced her, the phone dropped from her hands and Allison passed out onto the floor.

Accompanied by Horace Banks, Robin Page wasted no time in getting to the brownstone. Remembering that Allison had left the key to her apartment in her mailbox, he forced it open, and the two men bounded up the stairs by twos. When they opened the door, they found Allison on the floor in a pair of pajamas. She was out cold. Together, they lifted her and carried her to the bed. Horace felt for a pulse, while Robin prepared a cold compress in an attempt to revive her. As she came around, she could hear their voices in muffled tones.

"I knew there would be trouble," Robin was saying.

"Yes," Horace agreed. "That woman was the trouble."

"If I hadn't come to water the plants, we'd never have known she was here."

"It's a good thing we are abandoning the project."

"Abandon…the…" Allison's eyes flew open, and she reached a frail hand out to them.

"There, there." Horace Banks patted her hand tenderly. "Everything is going to be fine, Allison."

She raised her head as Robin propped up her pillows. "I think some color is returning to your cheeks," he said, smiling.

"She was here, wasn't she?" Allison accepted the glass of water Robin brought to her lips.

"Yes," he answered. "I found her experiencing color television in the living room."

"Her name is Lois."

"We know." It was Horace who replied. "She's the reason we have to abandon the project." He sat down on the edge of her bed, his face worn and tired. "Our experiment with you led us to assume the capsules only moved one back in time. This woman's appearance made us realize that moving through time could be accomplished in either direction, depending upon the chemistry and the desire of the person taking the pill. Destiny may certainly be playing a big part in the transition through time, at least in the case of you and Lois."

"What you don't know is that traveling in one's own time is very dangerous," Robin continued for the doctor. "This woman is alive in present time—and elderly. Her chance of survival is almost zero if two of her remain here."

"I tried to explain that to her."

"And from the looks of you, she's a real tough cookie," Horace offered. "I wouldn't be surprised if you had some internal damage. We should really get you to the hospital."

Allison did not argue. "Does the Lois of our time know she took this journey?"

The men looked at each other.

"No," Horace answered. "It's not likely she does. However, we can't be sure."

"Then I want to speak to her. Put me in the same hospital."

"Allison—"

"Please! Maybe I can stop her. Maybe I can prevent her from what she plans to do."

"Which is?" Robin asked.

"She wants to return to our time to kill herself—her *old* self."

CHAPTER TWENTY-FOUR

While Allison was being admitted, the doctors attempted to locate Lois. Without a last name, the hospital personnel were uncooperative. They looked through the admitting records and came up with eighteen women with the name Lois and took the list back to Allison's room.

"How are you feeling?" Robin asked, taking her hand into his.

"I've been better." She was sitting up in bed in a hospital smock. "I've got a few broken ribs, but I'll live. More importantly, did you find Lois?"

Horace handed her the list, and for the first time, Allison realized she never knew Lois's last name. Lois Allen. Lois Barrett. Lois Gimble. She traced down the list with a finger...Lois Lincoln.

"Oh, no!" Her finger stopped, the blood quickly draining from her face. "Lois Minetti! That's impossible! Johnny didn't marry her. Mrs. G. told me he never married because Ali never returned. This can't be!"

"I'm going to give her a sedative." Horace turned from Robin Page, reached into his medical bag for his syringe, and administered the sedative. "You changed all that when you went back the second time, Allison. Apparently she married John Minetti."

"Oh, God, what have I done?"

The serum worked quickly, and Allison drifted off into a deep sleep.

CHAPTER TWENTY-FIVE

When Allison woke it was two o'clock in the afternoon. Two hours and forty-eight years from now, she was supposed to be saying, "I do" to Johnny Minetti. The sedative had cheated her out of several hours. The young Lois may have already come and gone, leaving the old Lois dead in a hospital room. Slightly wavering, Allison eased her feet into her slippers and threw on the robe Robin Page had thoughtfully taken along to the hospital. The list of people named Lois lay on the table beside the bed, and Allison quickly scanned the page for a room number. Three twenty. As luck would have it, they were on the same floor, Lois's room in close proximity to the solarium.

Rounding several long and fortunately empty corridors, Allison stopped in front of number three twenty and slowly opened the door. The light by the bed was on, but Lois was asleep. Allison walked in and shut the door. Lois's hair was a dull gray; her body so big the hospital sheet did not cover her fully.

"Lois?" Allison questioned in a whisper. "Lois?" She touched a hand to the old woman. "Wake up, Lois."

The old woman opened her eyes slowly and gave a long sigh. "Who is it? Can't see a thing without my glasses."

Allison moved in closer and tightened her grip on Lois's hand. "It's me," she said.

"Who?" Lois attempted to sit up, but Allison gently pushed her back. "I need my glasses...the table...please."

Allison removed the heavy bifocals from their leather case and put them into her hands. Lois put them on and looked up.

"Ali?" she asked, raising her head from the pillow, her voice gruff from too many cigarettes. "It can't be. You're too young to be her." She sank back into the pillows. "Are you related by some chance?"

"Yes."

"That explains it then...Ali was so long ago."

"She sends her regards."

"Does she? That surprises me."

"Why?"

"I—"

"Has your husband visited you?"

Lois laughed a low, throaty laugh. "Husband? You mean the man I married, don't you?"

"Is there a difference?"

"A husband is someone who promises to love, honor, and obey. Promises to cherish you 'til death. I wouldn't call Johnny a husband."

"That's unfortunate."

"What do you want anyway? Can't you see I'm not well? If you're related to her, I want nothing to do with you. Leave me alone." With difficulty, Lois turned over on her side. "Please…just leave me alone."

"I'm here to prepare you, Lois. Lois?" She placed a hand on the old woman's shoulder. She was asleep. "Now what?" she asked aloud.

"Your guess is as good as mine, as Johnny would say."

The young Lois stood by the doorway dressed in a pair of cuffed dungarees and a navy blue blouse. "So that's what becomes of me, eh? I'm to believe that sorry old fat woman is me? That what I heard her tell you is true?"

Allison turned around. Young Lois was clutching the package of vials to her ample chest.

"Not a pretty sight is it? But you got your wish, Lois. You married Johnny."

Lois silently shook her head and walked further into the room. "Johnny did this to me?"

"You did it to yourself. You married a man who wasn't capable of returning your love." Allison sat down in the chair beside the bed and stared down at the aging, obese Lois. "This is how you'll wind up, Lois." Allison tightened the belt on her robe and looked over at the young Lois who stood still, fearful to move closer to her older self.

"You can change things. I changed history, so can you. You can use this knowledge to your advantage." Allison tried desperately to sound casual, but her words poured forth at a feverish pitch.

"You're trying to trick me!" Lois said, tightening her hold on the vials. "You want to scare me."

"I did not create the woman in this bed," Allison said, pointing. "You did that with no help from me."

"Then how can I change things?"

Allison swallowed hard and extended her hand to her nemesis. "Give me the vials."

"NO!"

"Lois, you know now that you shouldn't have stood in the way of Johnny's happiness…know you didn't live a loving and happy life with him. That knowledge is surely enough for you to change your plans and know you can't force someone to return your love. It wasn't meant to be!"

Lois looked down at the package and back up at Allison before sinking to the floor on her knees where she burst into tears.

"Oh, God, Ali, if you only knew…knew how much I love Johnny." She took a deep breath and wiped her eyes with the back of a hand. "All my life, Ali, that's how long I've loved John Minetti…all my life."

Allison got up from the chair and bent down beside Lois on the floor. "I do know, Lois. I also know how painful love can be." She placed a hand on her shoulder. "How old are you, Lois?"

Lois looked up, surprised. "What?"

"How old are you in 1944?"

"Older than Johnny, that's for sure," she sniffled. "I just had my thirtieth birthday."

Allison sighed loudly. "Thirty is still young enough to find someone. Maybe you've been holding out for Johnny too long. You need to—"

"What? Find someone to appreciate me? Fat chance!"

"You don't give yourself enough credit. You're a pretty girl, Lois."

"You think so?"

Allison nodded. "Too good for Johnny."

Lois got up from the floor and walked over to the mirror above the dresser, one hand smoothing a leg of her pants. Her eyes were slits when she turned to Allison. "And you aren't?"

"Some people are meant for each other. Look at the woman in that bed. Does she look like she's lived life with the mate God intended?"

Lois shook her head. "I guess not."

"Then help me get back to Johnny...help yourself get back to change your life."

Reluctantly, Lois handed the package of vials to Allison who blew out an audible sigh of relief.

"You'll get to your damn wedding, Ali, but what about me? I'm supposed to be a witness. I only just took one of those pills. I'm stuck here for another two days."

"If you'll help, I have an idea I think will work."

Lois accompanied Allison back to her room where Allison dialed Horace and Robin at ChemProbe. Insisting she felt better, she asked that they release her and meet at the brownstone.

"I found Lois, and she's willing to cooperate. I have a plan that might work." Hanging up, she walked to the small closet for her clothing.

"Who was that?" Lois asked curiously.

"The two doctors responsible for the capsules."

Lois sat on the bed. "Oh, yeah. I remember those guys. The young one's not too bad, if you know what I mean."

Allison smiled and shook her head. "Robin Page caught your eye, ha? Well, save yourself for the men in your own generation, okay?" She reached for the blouse on the hanger and winced, pain pulsating through her ribs.

"Let me." Lois hopped off the bed and helped Allison into her clothes. "I didn't think I hit you that hard."

"Yes, well, I wasn't prepared for that kind of confrontation. I'm a pacifist by nature."

"A what?"

"Never mind."

"What do you do for a living?" Lois asked while watching Allison comb her hair.

"I was head of public relations at ChemProbe, the company that manufactures the pills. I work with Doctors Banks and Page."

"Damn! Women have certainly come a long way. Bet you make a helluva lot of money. I took one look at your apartment and knew that much. You can afford to watch color movies in your own home!"

Allison laughed. "It was a decent job, I guess."

"You'd leave it all for Johnny? I wouldn't."

"If you truly loved him, no sacrifice would be too great."

"You think I'll meet someone when we go back to 1944?"

Allison put an arm around Lois's shoulders. "Lois, I not only know you will, I'm going to do my best to introduce you to someone deserving of you."

"Gee, thanks, Ali. That's nice of you, considering."

Allison smiled. "It is…considering."

CHAPTER TWENTY-SIX

Taking a cab back to the brownstone, Allison hustled Lois inside quickly, fearing Mrs. G. might open her door and see her old friend—young. At the top of the landing, she took out her key and opened the door, pushing Lois quickly inside. Lois zeroed in on the television and, turning it on, sat on the sofa, her feet propped up on the coffee table.

"I was going to say, make yourself comfortable, but I see there's no need." Allison smiled and shook her head. She might as well allow Lois the simple pleasure of television before they went back.

"This is incredible!" Lois was watching a rerun of *Roseanne*. "People are so…different. And this woman has no control over her kids. They all need the belt."

While Lois mesmerized herself in front of the tube, Robin Page and Horace Banks discussed her fate with Allison in the kitchen. The plan she revealed to them was simple enough. Horace, known for his successful experiments with subjects under hypnosis, would hypnotize Lois to forget the capsules, the journey, and even her animosity toward Allison. She would return to 1944 a wiser, and ultimately happier, woman.

"I have three considerations that might stand in the way of success," Horace pointed out. "Firstly, she has to be a willing subject. Secondly, there is no guarantee she will forget the journey…forever. And, more importantly, there is no guarantee that you will both return to 1944."

"That's a chance I'll have to take," Allison said while filling three mugs with coffee. "After all, there isn't much time you know."

"Anybody here have a cigarette?" Lois stood poised by the entrance to the kitchen.

"No, none of us smokes." It was Allison who answered. "Besides, we have to talk to you." She pulled out a kitchen chair. "Have a seat, Lois."

Lois sat down slowly, warily. Allison offered her a cup of coffee, but Lois waved it away. "Got anything stronger?"

Horace patted her hand. "I don't think that would be wise, my dear." He looked down at his watch. "We haven't much time, Dr. Page," he said formally.

"I've got two days!" Lois exclaimed in rebellion.

Robin Page got up and moved from the table. "I'll get the medical bag."

Horace nodded. Allison kept her eyes on Lois who was showing signs of uneasiness.

"Hey, what's going on?" Her eyes followed Robin. "Why does he need a medical bag?" She started to rise, but Allison put a hand gently on her shoulder.

"It's okay, Lois. You're in safe hands."

"You don't sound very convincing."

Allison knew she didn't. If anything, she sounded frightened. The capsule had almost failed before. What if it didn't work at all? What if she couldn't complete this final journey successfully? And, even if she did, would she remain in 1944, or might her system become immune to the pills, dooming her to… where? And that wasn't the worst scenario. There was also the strong possibility her journey would move forward; a dim prospect at best. She was certain of one thing: Lois would go back when her capsule wore off. Nineteen forty-four was Lois's time. She could still wind up marrying Johnny if Allison didn't make it back, and she would be aware of the unhappiness that lay ahead for her. No one would forget Ali, but she would be forgotten—to time.

"I would have preferred working in the lab," Horace said while administering a sedative to a once-frazzled Lois who now rested on the sofa. He withdrew the needle and pressed a cotton ball to the puncture.

"She has to be in this apartment," Robin reminded him. "Maybe we can move her to the bedroom."

"No," Allison interjected, her hands fluffing the pillows under Lois's groggy head. "In 1944 that room is Johnny's. We can't have Lois materialize there, it could frighten Frances and God only knows what Johnny's reaction would be."

"What makes you so sure Johnny's back in his own room?" Robin asked.

"I'm not sure. I just don't want to take any chances."

"Well someone could easily be in the living room."

Horace covered Lois with the blanket Allison handed him. "Well, she looks comfortable enough. We'll just have to pray no one is in the room when she returns. Keeping her sedated will be easy, but hypnotizing her…"

Robin kicked a hassock over and sat down. "We'll have to wait it out and hope she is a suggestive subject."

Horace nodded and turned to Allison. "I imagine you'll be leaving us now. You don't want to be late for your wedding." Horace made a small attempt at a smile. "God bless you, my dear. No matter what you encounter, embrace it with love." He reached a hand over to her, and Allison took it in her own with a squeeze.

Robin got up and handed Allison the package of vials. "We're going to miss you."

"Maybe we'll see each other again some day."

"Maybe."

Allison retired to the bedroom with a glass of water, popped open one of the vials, and swallowed. Her hands clasped tightly together, she said a little prayer before lying down on the bed.

CHAPTER TWENTY-SEVEN

Johnny Minetti was dressed in his tuxedo and a frantic Frances was hustling to open the door to their brownstone apartment.

"I just don't know where Ali could be!" Johnny looked down at his watch. It was already three o'clock. "We've done a thorough search, and we've reported the fact that both Ali and Lois are missing to Captain Ramsey. I don't know what else we can do." He loosened his tie and sat down in his chair, his fingers running through his thick hair in frustration. "I guess there isn't going to be a wedding."

"And why not?" Allison walked into the living room.

"Ali!" Johnny ran to her. "Where the hell have you been?" he shouted before pressing her to him in a strong hold. "We've been looking everywhere! You've got to stop disappearing on me."

Allison kissed him fully on the mouth. "I'm sorry."

"Ali! Where have you been?" Frances joined in the embrace.

"It doesn't matter." She gathered Frances's hands into her own while still in Johnny's embrace. "I found Lois. She got into a little trouble, but she's okay."

"Then I should go to her." Frances headed for the back door. Ali and Johnny followed.

"No!" Allison caught her hand. "She's sleeping… let her rest. Besides, you have to stand up for us at City Hall. You're my Maid of Honor, remember?"

Johnny looked down at his watch again. "Oh, God, that's right! We've got to get downtown, and we're cutting it close."

"Allison isn't even dressed yet!" Frances shook her head. "Come on, Ali, into the bedroom."

CHAPTER TWENTY-EIGHT

April 1994
For two years, Robin Page repeatedly returned to the scene of Allison's final disappearance. Each time he would venture up the steps of the brownstone and to Allison's third floor apartment. He never knocked; always losing his nerve while his fist was midway to touching the door. He knew she wasn't there, though for the life of him, the explanation was still one he found difficult to accept. Had things worked out for her? Or was she stuck in time somewhere, unable to find home? He and Horace had no way of knowing; there hadn't been time enough to devise a signal of communication—a way to let them know all was okay.

The usual derelicts and homeless people were nestled into their appointed spaces along the street, but there was a surprising amount of activity in front of the brownstone. Moving men were pushing out furniture and carpeting, and a For Rent sign dangled on a chain in front. "Apply Within, First Floor."

Elbowing his way past the movers, Robin ran up the steps and stood in front of the partially open door to the first floor apartment. "Anybody home?" he called.

"Can I help you?" A strikingly handsome man with a full head of white wavy hair answered the door. Tall and youthfully dressed in light blue pants and a Polo shirt, he smiled warmly.

"Arnold Palmer, right?" Robin couldn't help asking. "I've seen you on television," he jested.

"Sorry, but I have heard that many times before," the man apologized with a smile. "Can I help you?"

"I saw your sign out front. I work here in the city. The name's Robin Page." They shook hands.

"John Minetti. Come on in." He led Robin past several half-filled boxes and a rolled up carpet. "Excuse the mess. My sister was mugged a month ago, and she finally decided to let go of this place."

"I hope she's okay."

"Got away lucky. We packed her off to Florida and sunshine."

"Is this the apartment for rent?" Robin asked, looking around the bare living room, square spots where framed pictures had been, revealing the original paint.

"One of them. There's another on the third floor, slightly smaller." John continued to pack, wrapping some figurines in newspaper and stuffing them carefully into a box, his muscular arms lifting it and moving it to the side. "I'm not handling the rental, my wife is. She's especially attached to the house and very particular as to who rents here." He shouted to another room. "Honey! Come here, we have a potential tenant."

Allison McKay Minetti stepped carefully through the cluttered living room. She was still beautiful—her hair short and curly, framing her youthful face—her slim figure packed tightly into a pair of designer jeans and a denim shirt rolled up at the sleeves. When she saw Robin, her eyes widened and she smiled. There was immediate recognition between them.

"Yes, John?"

"This young man is looking to rent."

"Robin…Page," he said, introducing himself with hesitation, unable to look away from the familiar, vibrant eyes.

"Allison Minetti." She extended her hand. "Everyone calls me Ali."

Robin nodded, unable to find the voice he suddenly lost.

"I'll get our rental agreement," she said, pulling out a dresser drawer.

"I'd like to see the third floor apartment, too," Robin said finally.

"She's so efficient," John said.

"We're moving to Florida from Westchester for our fiftieth wedding anniversary."

Robin grinned nervously. "Fiftieth?"

"Long marriage and wouldn't trade a moment of it. She's a wonderful woman. A little head strong" he said, a twinkle in his eye.

"I don't doubt it," Robin mumbled, half to himself.

"Excuse me?" John asked as he continued to pack.

"I said, how about it?" He looked down at his watch. "I'm a bit pressed for time."

Allison grinned at his comment, picked up the master keys to the apartment along with a large, thick envelope. "Here we are." She came to John's side, and he put an arm around her slender waist and gave her a tender kiss.

"I'll show you the third floor apartment first," she said.

As they mounted the stairs together, Allison chattered without pause about the rooms, how much he would like living in the brownstone, and how long the place had been owned by the Minetti family. At the top, she stopped abruptly and handed him the key, folding it gently into the palm of his hand.

"Allison?" he asked softly.

"Open the door, Robin. You look as if you need to sit down."

Robin Page opened the door and walked in. Except for a few folding chairs in the kitchen, the apartment was empty. He sat down and watched Allison fill a paper cup with water. She handed it to him and sat down. He drank the water quickly, his hands shaking.

"I must have come by this place a hundred times in the last two years."

"How is the project going?" she asked suddenly.

"We abandoned it soon after Lois left us. I take it things turned out well for her? I can see they did for you."

"Yes. I introduced her to a friend of Johnny's, and they've been living a very content life together."

"No trouble from her?"

Allison shook her head. "If she remembers anything, she's done an excellent job of hiding it."

Robin looked up into her eyes. "It really is you, isn't it?"

Allison nodded and leaned in conspiratorially. "Aged well, haven't I?"

"It's…remarkable is what it is."

"You and Horace shouldn't have abandoned the project, Robin."

"Too many failed attempts. I was so disillusioned that I quit ChemProbe." He stopped speaking and stared at her for a long moment.

"The capsule works, Robin! It truly does work," she said seriously. "Just not for colds. Surely you and Horace accepted that as fact."

"Not really. The pill was unreliable. We had no way of knowing what it would do or where it would send a subject with no means to even communicate with them. It was much too risky to continue."

Allison got up and bent down to one of the cabinets, removed a strong box and handed it to Robin. "I lost the key. Take it to Horace and break it open."

"Why?"

"Because I lost the key, Robin! Can't you just once not take issue and just do as you are asked?" she said with slight annoyance.

Robin bit his lower lip and shrugged.

"There are several journals in the box," she continued. "Each one details my experience with the capsules, which I might add, I don't seem to need much any more. I forgot to take them a couple of times and I'm still here!" She was smiling again. "I have a supply for emergency," she added quickly. "There are photos in the box, as well." She leaned in closer. "Take it to Horace Banks and, please, use it wisely." She got up from the chair and turned to face him. "One more thing. A business card is in the box. It was given to me in 1944 by a woman named Nina Davenport, and she is someone in your time who is helping other time travelers with their journeys."

Robin Page stared down at the large strong box in front of him as he would an alien from outer space. Allison walked out of the kitchen, stopped just short of the entrance, and turned around.

"I've handed you a heavy burden, Dr. Page. Had you not shown up today, I had every intention of mailing it to ChemProbe. Don't disappoint me," she said, walking to the front door.

"What about the apartment?" Robin asked, jumping up from the folding chair and rushing to catch up with her. "Is it still for rent?"

Allison gave him a queer look. "If you want it, certainly." She opened the envelope and handed him a rental agreement. "But why would you want to live here when you have a fine apartment already?"

"An excuse to keep in touch, I imagine." He looked down at his feet shuffling self-consciously beneath him. "You may not have been aware of it, but in my own way I really cared, I mean, care, for you. I always hoped you would come back."

"Oh, Robin, that's the nicest thing you've ever said to me." She shook her head. "But I've turned back the clock too many times already. I like it right where I am…and where I was."

"But, I wonder, was it right to play God and change history the way you did? It's dangerous to tempt fate. There's so much I want to know."

"And I've written it all down for you in the journals."

"But I want to hear it from your own lips, Allison!"

She touched a hand to his as he remembered his mother having done so many times. "Get on with your life and encourage Horace Banks to resume his experiments with the capsules. We are all put on this earth for a purpose. I have fulfilled mine and intend to retire to Florida with my husband."

"We've come to the conclusion that you were an isolated incident, Allison. So was Lois."

"I can't tell you and Horace what to do, Robin. All I ask is that you read my journals and take their contents into consideration." She patted his hand again. "Make yourself busy again in that lab. Try to get your job back." With a playful wink, Allison opened the door. "Maybe one day you'll take a sentimental journey of your own."

The End

Made in the USA
Charleston, SC
10 October 2014